"I ain't never gonna wait behind no Injun again..."

Barrett's head turned. Three of the men who had gathered and complained in the saloon the previous evening were there. Barrett said, "You're standing behind one now."

The men looked around the store, puzzled. They didn't see any Indians.

"What the hell you talkin' about, blue-leg?"

"I'm part Indian," said Barrett. "Can't you tell? I'm taller than you, stronger than you, better looking than you. What else could I be?"

Unfortunately, Private Barrett wasn't bigger and stronger than all three. They took his size into account, added the Army uniform, noted the absence of any obvious Army backup, and after totaling up all these considerations, they started swinging...

EASY COMPANY

EASY COMPANY

AND THE WHITE MAN'S PATH

JOHN WESLEY HOWARD

A JOVE BOOK

Requests for permission to make copies of any part of the work should be mailed to: Permissions, Jove Publications, Inc., 200 Madison Avenue, New York, NY 10016

First Jove edition published May 1981

First printing

Printed in the United States of America

Jove books are published by Jove Publications, Inc., 200 Madison Avenue, New York, NY 10016

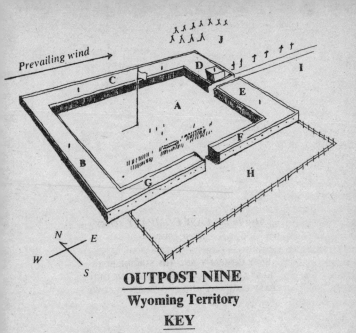

Prevailing wind →

N E
W
S

OUTPOST NINE
Wyoming Territory
KEY

A. Parade and flagstaff

B. Officers' quarters ("officers' country")

C. Enlisted men's quarters: barracks, day room, and mess

D. Kitchen, quartermaster supplies, ordnance shop, guardhouse

E. Suttler's store and other shops, tack room, and smithy

F. Stables

G. Quarters for dependents and guests; communal kitchen

H. Paddock

I. Road and telegraph line to regimental headquarters

J. Indian camp occupied by transient "friendlies"

INTERIOR   OUTSIDE

OUTPOST NUMBER NINE
(DETAIL)

Outpost Number Nine is a typical High Plains military outpost of the days following the Battle of the Little Big Horn, and is the home of Easy Company. It is not a "fort"; an official fort is the headquarters of a regiment. However, it resembles a fort in its construction.

The birdseye view shows the general layout and orientation of Outpost Number Nine; features are explained in the Key.

The detail shows a cross-section through the outpost's double walls, which ingeniously combine the functions of fortification and shelter.

The walls are constructed of sod, dug from the prairie on which Outpost Number Nine stands, and are sturdy enough to withstand an assault by anything less than artillery. The roof is of log beams covered by planking, tarpaper, and a top layer of sod. It also provides a parapet from which the outpost's defenders can fire down on an attacking force.

one

An uneasy quiet lay over Outpost Number Nine. Mr. Lo was behaving himself for the time being, but a yearning for peace did not seem to run very deep in the Indians of 1877. And as far west as the Wyoming Territory, where Outpost Number Nine was located, it hardly extended below the surface.

Such were the sentiments of Easy Company's first sergeant, Ben Cohen, a longtime veteran of the Indian Wars. Easy Company was a contingent of mounted infantry, sometimes called 'dragoons' by the public and press, but that was a generic term loosely applied to damn near any soldier that rode a horse, and it was therefore not a very accurate designation. Either way, Easy had to be ready to mount up at a split second's notice and ride off to restore order. Thus it behooved (a favorite Cohen word) a good top kick to keep his men on their toes. Cohen did this by keeping them so busy—regrading roads, stringing telegraph wire, repairing fortifications, scrubbing and polishing everything that didn't move, collecting and laying in about twenty years' supply of wood, toting "honey buckets"—that riding into battle would come as a welcome relief.

Cohen came out of the orderly room and stood looking over the parade, automatically scanning the outpost, *his* outpost, as

1

if a wall might have fallen down since morning assembly. One hadn't, nor was it likely to, unless the Indians acquired artillery.

The parade was empty, save for a crew digging a new latrine pit near the enlisted barracks. Poor beggars'd be taking the sun full now. Cohen glanced at the sun. It was getting on toward noon of an early summer day. Beginning to feel the heat, Cohen strode off toward the distant pit detail.

The detail had been drawn from Mr. Allison's Third Platoon. Cohen could see the broad, bare, heaving shoulders of Private Jeremy Enright, formerly James Evinrude. Getting closer, he distinguished the bullet-headed Private Moore, the new recruit, Private Barrett, the loudmouthed, brawling Private Popper, and another new recruit named John Gillies, an undersized runt from the New York slums, whom the men disparagingly called Weasel. That was five. Cohen thought he'd detailed six. Then he saw Private Kazmaier, a man of low intelligence but high cunning, emerge from the mess toting a bucket of water. Cohen guessed it had probably taken Kazmaier a half-hour to get the water.

"How's it going?" Cohen asked, letting them know he hadn't forgotten about them.

"Real peachy, Sarge."

Cohen eyed Moore. Silly remarks were his trademark. "Be sure to make it deep enough. But stop when you hit water."

"How far down's the water table?" asked Enright, an ex-farmer who was curious about such things.

"You'll find out." Cohen watched Kazmaier gently set the bucket down. "Why don't you men take a break, refresh yourselves. Let Kazmaier dig for a while."

They scrambled out and Kazmaier promptly leaped in, where he dug with unusual zest until Cohen was safely back in the orderly room.

Letting his spade drop, Kazmaier complained, "Hell, you'd think we was niggers, the way he makes us go in this sun." His pale blue eyes glared from his nut-brown face.

"You *do* look kinda dark, Kaz. Gittin' darker, too," Moore observed.

"Yeah, but at least *I* started out *white*. *Barrett's* the one that's got a lot of explainin' to do."

Barrett eyed Kazmaier narrowly. Barrett was tall, well built, and reasonably good-looking. But his skin was naturally darker than most, his hair thick and black, his cheekbones high and angled, his nostrils very slightly flared, and his lips thicker and browner than most. He did appear to be, in Kazmaier's favorite phrase, a "mongrelized bastard."

Barrett's eyes were mere slits now. "I told you bastards, I got Injun blood way back somewhere. Hell, I *hate* niggers."

Kazmaier, undaunted, smiled nastily. "An' Weasel too . . ."

"Goddammit!" squawked the narrow-featured Gillies, "I'm Armenian, an' Turk besides."

Barrett wished he'd thought of that.

"'Cept Weasel's such a runt," continued Kazmaier. "I never seen a nigger runt."

"An' I never seed a blue-eyed asshole," cried Gillies, reaching for a spade handle.

"Whaddaya think they do down South?" interjected Moore, trying to smooth things over.

"Whaddaya mean?" demanded Kazmaier.

"I mean the army. They're supposed to be all niggers down there. Who do you reckon digs their latrines—Injuns?"

"The officers too?"

"Too? Too what?"

"They niggers too?"

"Naw. They're white."

"Bet they're downright ecstatic about *that* command."

"But it's not just because of the coloreds," said Enright, joining the discussion as he climbed back down into the pit, "who ain't supposed to be all that bad as fighters. Naw, it's something more than that." He started digging. "This handgun we got, the Scoff? There ain't all that many of them around, and I hear we only got them because the army got a bargain. Or that's what they say. But it's a good gun. Smith & Wesson makes good guns. And the *real* reason it ain't admired is that the designer, Schofield, was once an officer with the Tenth Cav—that's one of the colored outfits—and the big brass don't think much of them officers, don't like to single 'em out for any kind of notice."

"How come? Schofield prob'ly didn't have no choice who he commanded. Army'll screw you, give 'em half a chance."

"Maybe so, but there's some that think an officer should resign his commission 'fore taking a command like that. Like a white officer shouldn't have to command coloreds."

3

"Someone's gotta," said Moore.

"What for?" demanded Kazmaier. "Let them bastards pick cotton, that's all they're good for."

"Like I said, the Ninth and Tenth ain't supposed to be bad," observed Enright mildly. "And I hear tell a lot of cowboys are colored."

"So what? So're some Injuns. An' a lot of them greasy brown bastards from down Mexicali way. That don't make it right." Kazmaier found himself in rare possession of a principle. "Anyway, how do you know all that stuff about Schofield and the niggers?"

"Lieutenant Kincaid," replied Enright.

"Oh, yeah? You and him is buddies, that it?" Kazmaier asked.

"Nope," said Enright, heaving a load of dirt at Kazmaier.

"*I* would've," said Barrett.

"You would've what?" asked Popper.

"Resigned my commission. I've had somethin' to do with niggers in my time—"

"I'll bet you have," sneered Kazmaier.

"—An' there ain't nothin' lower. The only thing worse'n an Injun is a nigger." He seemed excessively worked up, his neck corded, eyes roving wildly. "If'n I was down South watchin' that Tenth Cav go up against Mr. Lo, I wouldn't hardly know who to root for. Hellfire, it'd sure be tough to choose."

"Yeah," said Popper, matching Kazmaier's sneer and measuring Barrett. Popper liked to fight, to brawl, it was about all he knew. He didn't always win, but he always came back for more. Barrett was a new man, a big man, and thus far untested. Popper couldn't resist. "*I've* met a few coloreds in my day and I don't think much of them either, but they're better'n some—"

"They're *all* scum," insisted Barrett.

"—They're one hell of a lot better'n some what won't admit they're niggers, what call themselves 'part Injun.' How's that for bein' colored—colored *yella!*"

Barrett thought it over, thinking about what Popper meant, thinking the other men knew what he meant, maybe even agreed, even Enright. "Get up, Popper," he growled.

"I don't git up fer no nigger *or* no Injun."

"Then take it settin' down," said Barrett, and strode toward him.

Popper was on his feet in a flash, but not fast enough to avoid a hard left. He staggered backwards, shaking it off. The bastard's a lefty, he thought. That's his good hand.

It wasn't. Barrett feinted another left hook, but then lifted Popper clear off the ground with a right, dug up into his belly.

Sergeant Cohen had heard the clamor and came barreling out of the orderly room. The first sergeant, the company's undisputed Top Fist, loved a good fight.

Getting near, though, he saw that this one wasn't so good. The big recruit, Barrett, was making mincemeat out of Popper, filling Popper's big, loud mouth with knuckles. And doing it fast. Cohen would have preferred a longer, more drawn-out engagement.

Cohen exchanged glances with Private Enright, another man who fought little because he fought so well. Just the week before, in town, Cohen had watched Enright do a bullwhacker the way Barrett was doing Popper.

Popper suddenly shot backwards and pitched into the pit, where Enright caught him. Enright got a good hold on Popper and heaved him back out, where the man lay unconscious in the dust.

"Moore, Kazmaier, Gillies," said Cohen, "haul Popper back to the barracks." He shook his head. "He better start saving his fighting for Mr. Lo. As for you, Barrett, I don't know how this started, but Popper—"

"Popper started it, Sarge," said Gillies.

"Popper's a nigger-lover," added Barrett.

Cohen gave Barrett a look, then said, "That ain't necessary."

"The big guy really tore up Popper's ass, didn't he?" said a young, nasal voice.

They all looked to where a boy stood. Fifteen, sixteen years old, he was small, but not much smaller than Gillies, upon whom he'd fastened his eyes. "You're Weasel, aintcha?"

"Who the hell let you in *this* time, Billy?" demanded Cohen.

"Who's he, Sarge?" snarled Gillies. "Dependent kid?"

"This kid? Hell, no, look at him, scrawnier than hell and near dressed in rags. He's from a town near fifty miles from here. Scares up a pony, rides it over, bothers the bejesus out of us. Wants to be an effin' soldier. All he *is*, though, is a pain in the ass. C'mon, now, Billy, beat it. Or go over and beg somethin' at the sutler's. An' the rest of you get this clown Popper inside before he roasts to death."

They dragged poor Popper into the barracks with Billy right behind, as if Cohen had never spoken to him. As they all disappeared into the barracks, Weasel could be heard yelling, "For Chrissakes, kid, beat it!"

"Kid's a real pest," said Cohen. "Always around, but as far as I can tell he don't have shit for a family, so . . ."

Enright figured that hardly anyone out there at Outpost Nine, in the middle of Wyoming, had "shit for a family." If they had, they probably wouldn't be there.

"You two finish this hole, it's near done anyway," said Cohen. "I got plans for those other fellers. They're gonna wish . . ." But he turned and walked off without finishing his threat.

"How come he's sore at them?" wondered Barrett.

Enright was silent.

"Huh?" prompted Barrett.

"He just gets sore sometimes, that's all. He's the first sergeant, he's allowed."

"Don't seem fair."

Enright's head was down and he kept it down.

"I said it don't seem fair," Barrett repeated.

"Oh, he's fair about anything important. Now, are you gonna dig or think about what a great fighter you are?"

"I looked good, huh?" Barrett said, but there was no response.

Barrett dug. They both dug. Barrett kept making friendly overtures to Enright and kept being ignored. A look of hurt began to come over his face.

They soon had the hole completed and they climbed out.

"Enright? What's wrong?" Hell, a man could live alone, draw upon his own resources, and do all right if he had to, but not in the army. You had to have at least *one* buddy. "I wanna be friends," Barrett almost whined.

"I'm not sure I want to be friends with you," muttered Enright.

"But . . . but why?"

Enright looked at him, then reached out and started poking his chest with his finger for emphasis as he said, "Because I think you were wrong back there. Wrong *then*, and wrong, *period*."

"About what?"

6

"About coloreds," said Enright simply, mopping his brow and pushing his graying hair back. Enright was in his thirties, overage for a private. He'd fought in the War, mustered out, gone home to Maine, and then watched his family and all its branches wither and die. The last one, his son, had been killed in a fight and Enright had killed the killer. Then he'd rejoined the army. The law had come after him, found him, but then decided they didn't want him after all. They'd told him to change his name and let him stay on at Outpost Nine. He'd changed it, to Jeremy Enright, and didn't mind the change. He figured many of the men out there had something to hide and weren't using the names they were born with.

"I've seen a lot more than you have, Barrett, of life, of war . . . of *men*. I've known a number of coloreds, fought alongside some, and there were a few I wouldn't mind sidin' to hell and back, proud to call 'em my friends."

Barrett was watching Enright steadily, closely.

"And I'd never seen a colored," continued Enright, "till I was over twenty, so it's not like I was raised with 'em. There are good ones and bad ones, just like anyone, and you're a fool to think the way you do."

Enright was one of the few men that Barrett held in high regard. Sure, he admired Matt Kincaid and Captain Conway—and even Sergeant Cohen—but the men he was placing Enright among were the men he lived with, slept with, ate with, pissed alongside, the mostly dirty but mainly stupid enlisted men.

He reached out and touched Enright, who almost pulled away but didn't. Barrett's face softened, and a strange look came into his eyes.

"I was born on the twenty-sixth of April," said Barrett slowly, in a monotone, "in Fredericksburg, Virginia. That was the first time. There were thirteen children in my family, seven sons and six daughters. I was the third oldest. Had me an older sister and an older brother. The *second* time I was born, I was twelve years old, it was in 1866. And I've studied the language, I can speak it, I can talk with the Absaroka. . . ."

Enright listened closely, partly out of courtesy but also because it sounded so strange. Not just the words but the delivery. Had the sun gotten to the tall, black-haired man? His eyes certainly had a fevered look. Maybe Popper'd gotten a blow in that no one had seen. . . .

Absaroka. Where had he heard that before?

"Does that mean anything to you?" asked Barrett, his eyes slowly focusing on Enright.

"Other than that you're twenty-three years old, no."

This time Barrett looked like he was working up a full head of steam. He opened his mouth . . . but then the two of them saw a strange thing approaching. Actually it wasn't all that strange, just the large, portable, wooden latrine that was headed their way, carried by six grinning privates. What was so funny about carrying a latrine?

"The hole's finished, ain't it?" asked one of the porters, and Enright nodded. "Don't fall in," he said pleasantly, "or we'll have to toss you a rope."

"Haw-haw-haw," intoned another porter.

They placed the latrine snugly down over the hole and then, without a word, marched off. They went as far as the barracks but didn't enter; instead they hung around out front, keeping a sly watch on the latrine.

Enright saw them there, and wondered what was going on. But Barrett took no similar notice. He'd gotten that look back in his eyes. He was far away.

Enright studied him for a long while, then finally asked, "You all right?"

Barrett snapped out of it, blinking and shaking his head. "Yeah, I'm fine. But . . ." He took a deep breath. "But what you said before . . ." He was giving something one hell of a lot of thought. "Look, there's something no one knows, *no one,* and I probably shouldn't tell you, but I trust you. You're not like the rest. You're older, you're sensible, an' you've got to understand that when I was talking about"—his lips compressed—"about niggers before, sounding the way I did, it's . . . it's because I'm one-quarter colored myself."

"What?!"

"Shhhhh!" Barrett's eyes practically popped from his head. Enright blinked and sagged against the latrine.

"I guess that makes me a mulatto," Barrett concluded.

"Jeez," oozed Enright, "I guess so. You do mean *colored* colored."

Barrett nodded. "Or maybe I'm a quadroon."

Enright thought that was a dance they did down around New Orleans. "But why, Barrett? How come you're tryin' to be white?"

8

"You know why. The way I talked before is the way most white men talk about colored folk. I couldn't take it. Not without having to fight. An' how do you think I'd look, riding with the Tenth Cav?"

"Well, hell, I don't see what you're so goddamned worked up about. You *look* white enough to me, 'spite of what that asshole Kazmaier says."

"But that's the thing. I'm not. It's a lie. And it's tearing me apart. Now, I've heard talk of how hard it is for the Indian to follow the white man's path. And I've also read where a white man can become an Indian but an Indian can't become a white man."

"What's that supposed to mean?"

"Dunno, exactly. You figure it out. Can't civilize an Injun, maybe. But I've got the same problem. I've chosen the white man's path—"

"Sure have," commented Enright, recalling the earlier racial outbursts.

"—But it's not easy. I'm not sure I can do it. Maybe I need help." He looked hard at Enright. "And then there's something else, a calling I have. I hear voices. . . ."

"What?" Enright looked around. He didn't hear anyone.

"In my head. I hear them in my head."

"What do they say?"

Barrett only smiled.

"Like that stuff before, the twenty-sixth of April and Fredericksburg and stuff like that?" Enright said.

Barrett stared at him, slightly astonished. "*You* hear the same voices too?"

"No, dammit. That's what *you* said, just before."

"*I* didn't say anything," said Barrett soothingly, as if to imply that Enright was mad and had to be treated gently. Then Barrett got that faraway look again.

Here it comes, thought Enright. "Look, Jeff—that's your name, isn't it? Jeff?—let's head for the mess and see if Dutch has got some fresh coffee."

"Black soup."

"What? But Barrett said no more. Damn. Probably some special colored saying. Enright hung his head. How come Barrett had to tell *him* all that stuff?

The two men walked off toward the mess.

The men outside the barracks watched them go, their faces,

9

for some reason, glum with disappointment. Then they watched little Billy harass Weasel Gillies, following him in and out of the barracks.

"Them two deserve each other. Which one's worse, do you figger?"

"Kid's probably a thief."

"And Weasel ain't? He'd steal his mother's crutch."

"How do you know?"

"I know them kind. I been to the cities, I know what kind of scum grows up there."

"Don't grow very tall, it seems."

As they laughed about that, the door to the latrine slowly swung open. And then an Indian face appeared, or a face grotesquely smeared with garish pigment to resemble that of a bloodthirsty brave hot on the warpath—a presence of dubious comfort, if not outright shock, to anyone seeking relief inside the latrine.

The "warrior" looked about, determined that Enright and Barrett were gone, and then leaped from the latrine. The paint on his face masked any expression, but as he hustled toward the barracks he began squawking like crazy.

two ──────────────────────

White Moccasin and his people had moved onto the
land reserved for the Crow Nation the previous fall. Located
in the southeastern quarter of Montana, it was bordered to the
west and north by the Yellowstone River, to the south by
Wyoming, and to the east . . . well, that was sort of vague. It
was a small sector of the great area that had once been the
hunting ground of the Crow Nation. It lacked, certainly, the
large parts of Wyoming that had once been theirs, but if they
were going to follow the white man's ways, it was right that
they should share their land with their brothers, brothers at
whose side they, alone among the Plains tribes, had fought.

But it was hard. The buffalo were gone, and with them the
great hunts, the "surrounds." Their horses were scarce, which
was galling for a people who measured themselves through the
acquisition and possession of horses. They no longer battled
their Sioux and Blackfoot enemies, save at the side of white
soldiers. They lived on handouts from the Indian agency situated on the Yellowstone between them and Bozeman or Fort
Ellis. They were supposed to grow food, but had no knowledge
of planting, except for tobacco.

The Crow medicine men were tobacco planters. In those
men were invested the supernatural and prophetic powers that
accrue to medicine men. And those powers called for a tobacco-
planting ceremony, with traditional rites and site. The site was
usually located on the Wind River at the base of the Wind
River Mountains. But the Wind River was located in Wyoming,
beyond their reach. In the Season of Green Grass, just past,

11

White Moccasin had in fact conducted a tobacco planting on the reservation, but it was not the same.

Yes, the white man's way was proving hard.

Two soldiers rode among the tipis and sod huts of White Moccasin's Crow. They were Private Pete Rasmussen and Corporal Ed Mulberry. They were both with Colonel Nelson Miles's Fifth Mounted Infantry, at Fort Keogh. Mulberry had previously spent time with Outpost Nine's Easy Company, and had there proved what a poor field soldier he was. Transferred out, to save his sanity more than his life, the spindly, studious man had found himself attached to Miles's belligerent outfit. Not in a combat role, though. Rather as a specialist in Indian affairs and culture. Not that he knew as much about Indians firsthand, but he'd read enough to fill a tipi.

The War Department seemed to be curious about who it was they were exterminating, probably to help them do the job better. Mulberry had first thought he'd enjoy a transfer to the Bureau of Indian Affairs—the name sounded right—but that was before he learned there was no love lost between the BIA and the War Department, and that neither was a friend to the red man.

"They're having it rough," said Corporal Mulberry.

"Looks okay to me," said Private Rasmussen, whose sharp, quick eyes masked a dense brain. "Quiet," he added. "Just the way I like them."

"Beaten," said Mulberry. "Dying out. And they know it. Their shoulders don't slump like that 'cause they're happy."

"They got shelter—and food."

"The huts are adequate. Barely. And the tipis . . . they used to use great, thick buffalo pelts. Now they use army canvas. Probably sold the skins for whiskey. The Crow never used to be big drinkers, but they're catching on."

Rasmussen looked around warily.

"And I'll bet all those tipis look the same to you," Mulberry surmised. He was ready to give Rasmussen the full Indian Lore treatment.

Rasmussen looked. "They *are* all the same."

"I mean between Crow and Sioux and Cheyenne."

"Well, hell, if I got to see 'em all together . . ."

"For one thing, the Sioux and Cheyenne tipis are a little shorter, and the Sioux tilt more to the rear than the Cheyenne,

12

and the Crow hardly tilt at all. But the biggest difference is that the Sioux and Cheyenne use a three-pole foundation while the Crow use four. You can see there"—he pointed—"those four poles that are joined just below where the rest of the poles cross? Laid against them?"

"So? How's that important?"

"You can tell, from way off, who's in a village."

"Gotcha. Me Crow, them Sioux short tipi, me kill."

Mulberry smiled. "Only if you were sure you could attack without risking any of your warriors."

"You mean unless you were sure you could win."

"No. A war party that returns with no scalps, no coups, but no loss of life is honored more than a war party that comes back with ten scalps but has lost warriors. *That's* when you see the fingers fly."

"Hm?" grunted Rasmussen, but Mulberry only smiled.

"As for food," Mulberry went on, "the food they get is no bargain, that's number one. Number two, they hand it out to individuals, individual families. But in a free tribe, one that's taking care of itself, the chief or tribal council would be in charge of distribution."

"So?"

"So, what they're trying to do is destroy the red man's customs and tradition. Change their food, their clothes, their habits, destroy their gods. Make them white."

"Don't sound like you like it much."

"There's nothing much to like about it. But also nothing much that can be done. This is the way it is and will be. They'll have to change. Sink or swim."

Rasmussen looked around for water.

Chief White Moccasin moved slowly toward the big council tipi. It was the Season of Yellow Grass, but a breeze blew and he felt chilled as he never had before. All things were bad. His cotton pants were too big and baggy, yet too cluttered in the crotch where, beneath pants, he wore his breechclout. His shirt was also too large. He'd been given the clothes, and he thought the Americans meant well, but they had wrong ideas about the size of his people.

Maybe he was smaller. He *felt* smaller. How would his war bonnet fit? It had sixty eagle feathers. Thirteen eagles had died to fashion his bonnet. Each eagle had required a religious

13

ceremony and much perseverence. Patience atop a lofty pinnacle or in a covered pit. But White Moccasin was a man of great patience. And the war bonnet was greatly prized, worth many, many bottles of whiskey, many picks and shovels, many pants for fat Americans. He knew that. Americans had tried to buy his war bonnet. And he would not sell. But he thought that if he put the bonnet on now, it would slide down over his head to rest on his shoulders, masking his face, blinding him. Which was right. He felt small and like a blind man.

He entered the large tipi. Members of the tribal council awaited him. There were six, including himself: Lame Dog, Spotted Elk, Buffalo Hump, Little Deer, and Leaf That Cries. They were all younger than White Moccasin and were warriors, war chiefs. Or had been. Now they were like White Moccasin.

White Moccasin, whose medicine was strong, had for many, many seasons led the tribe, guided them, advised them, but only in peace. He did not plan their battles, nor did he wage them, and had not since the time his hair was solid black. He was the tribe's chief counsel, their father, but the sons fought. But it was like that with many tribes. Joseph, chief of their friends, the Nez Perce, despite his fearsome, warlike reputation occupied a role much the same as White Moccasin's.

He sat, sighing, the sullen faces telling him all he wanted to know.

"This should be a war council," said Spotted Elk. "Instead we meet to hear who went hungry."

"No one went hungry," said White Moccasin with his renowned patience. Spotted Elk said the same thing every time they met. But he was right. Why *did* they meet?

Buffalo Hump said, "Today the agent asked me where was *Mrs.* Hump? What did he mean?"

"He meant well. The American gives his name to his wives." He gave it some more thought. "Where *was* she?"

"Which one?" cried Buffalo Hump, exasperated. "You know I have five."

White Moccasin frowned. "And you know that is wrong. The Americans want you to have only one. We have spoken of this matter before."

"I cannot choose," was Buffalo Hump's doleful confession. "They all work hard. Cook, weave, wash..."

"And now at last they *can* wash. This white season past,

14

waughh!" Little Deer gave vent to several more guttural exclamations.

"Listen to us!" burst out Lame Dog, getting to his feet and standing tall. "We sound like women."

At least they didn't look like them. Lame Dog, and the rest of the council, were all well-proportioned, handsome men. And the Crow men, in general, were known to be among the most imposing of the entire Indian race. Truly noble.

"I've seen some ugly Injun women before, Corporal," said Rasmussen, scowling, "but these here take the cake."

Mulberry had become accustomed to Rasmussen's generally unreliable powers of observation. But in this case—"You're quite right. It's a documented anomaly that while both sexes of a common race, or tribe, *should* exhibit the same range of good or bad looks, the Crow do not. Many who have studied Indians have written that as much as the Crow men are uncommonly good-looking, the women are uncommonly ugly. And the men don't seem to care. They seem to have no notion of female beauty . . . or at least they don't have a *white* notion of female beauty."

Rasmussen's expression seemed to say, *"What other kind is there?"*

A woman walked past, carrying a tub of water. Mulberry watched her. "It's easier now that it's warm. They never washed much before they came here. Cleaned themselves and the skins they wore with white clay. Now there's no white clay and they have to wash cotton clothes. Which, of course, is not *that* bad. But in the winter, when they heat water to wash clothes, the hut or tipi fills with steam and they open it up to let the steam out and the snow blows in and the ground freezes."

Rasmussen shuddered involuntarily. Then his quick, sharp eyes opened wide. And not for the first time. He'd been watching the woman with the tub, too. "Corporal, there's something else I've noticed. . . ."

Mulberry eyed him, smiling in anticipation.

"I notice a lot of these people, not just the women—though they seem worse—but a lot got fingers missin'. That some kinda disease? *Leppersee?*" He was ready to kick his horse into motion and get the hell out of there.

"No, that's just a custom. When a person's killed, especially

15

a warrior, they go into terrible mourning. And in order not to forget their grief, they cut off a piece of finger." He grinned briefly at Rasmussen's horror. "Just a joint's worth. A reminder. And it's usually just the immediate family of the slain warrior that does it. But if someone like a chief is killed, then there's mourning all over and fingers fall like rain."

"That's really . . . really . . . stupid," Rasmussen managed.

"The way they do it," explained Mulberry, "is they lay their hand down, place a knife carefully over the joint, and then hit the knife with a piece of wood."

"How many hands they *got?*" It sounded to Rasmussen as though at least three were involved.

"Of course, sometimes, in an excess of zeal, they just whack away at the finger with a knife, cut a finger off between joints, and when that heals it leaves a piece of bone sticking out. They smear the blood from the finger on their faces, and they're careful in that they never cut the thumb and forefinger of the left hand or the thumb, forefinger, and middle finger of the right. That's so they can still handle a bow. Or a gun."

"What if they're left-handed?"

Mulberry made a face.

"You ever seen them do it?" Rasmussen pressed.

"I should say not."

"How do you know, then?"

"I've read about it. A man named Denig published some material. And then there's also something called the Culbertson manuscript in Missouri, handwritten. It's owned by the Culbertsons but no one knows who wrote it."

"Don't you do nothin' but read?"

"Then there's Beckwith, or Beckwourth. He wrote an autobiography, sort of, or he told it and a man named Bonner wrote it. Beckwith was a trapper who became a Crow war chief. Imagine that, a white man becoming an honest-to-God Crow war chief. Except, of course, he wasn't all white . . ."

"Injun?"

"The Crow thought so. Someone told them Beckwith was a Crow babe that had been stolen by the Sioux, but that he'd finally escaped and grown up to become a white trapper. The Crow are very gullible. They'll believe anything, especially if it smacks of the supernatural."

"Ain't nothin' supernatural 'bout smackin' off fingers."

"But Beckwith was really French, American, and some

16

Negro. A mulatto, using the broad definition."

"Them Crow *will* believe anything, won't they?"

"Beckwith had some pretty wild tales, a lot of them lies most likely, but a lot true. And *he* never said the Crow women were ugly."

"Figgers. I mean, he was colored. . . . But, gee, Corporal, Crow's kind of an ugly name anyway. Ugly bird, too. Figgers they might be ugly. Women, anyway. But some of them other names, they're *funny*. I heard one—Sits Down Spotted. Now what kinda name is that?"

"They're *different*, I grant you, but just to keep the record straight, Crow's not their name. They never call themselves that. Their Indian name, Absaroka, just means 'flying bird.' In English, they call themselves Sparrowhawk. The Sioux probably convinced the whites to call them Crow. And when you call them Crow, they respond, they've gotten used to it.

"But when it comes to names, you're right, sort of. One of the greatest Crow chiefs was called Rotten Belly. But sometimes they make sense. Chief Long Hair never cut his hair and kept the broken pieces pasted to the live pieces so it kept getting longer. Got to about eight, ten feet, maybe longer. Kept it rolled up in two balls in front of him when he was riding.

"And when you combine that with the way they do their hair—cut it so that there's a four-inch bang in front, and then that's pasted so it stands straight up—"

"Hey, yeah, I seen that."

"Just like any other white man," said Mulberry, and Rasmussen smiled hesitantly, not sure Mulberry was joking.

Lame Dog was seated again. But his left arm was outstretched and a knife was poised over his left wrist joint, resting on the skin.

"Do not be foolish, Lame Dog," said White Moccasin, more in sorrow than anger, for he understood.

"Brothers," cried Lame Dog, his handsome features contorted, "strike this knife with a strong bough. I am a warrior no longer, I am a *man* no longer, I need them not."

Naturally, no one made a move to grant his request. But all were shaken and knew what was in his heart.

"I hear the buffalo have gone to the mountains," said Leaf That Cries, "where they wait for us."

"Where there is much land," argued Lame Dog. "More than

17

plenty for the Americans *and* us. I have seen land empty as far as the eye can see. You too have seen it, my brothers. The Americans cannot want it *all*."

"He wants us here," said White Moccasin, "on this land."

"Then the Americans do not know the land is there."

"The Americans know. The red-haired chief told them." The red-haired chief that White Moccasin referred to was William Clark, of Lewis and Clark, a man the Crow Nation had almost worshipped and who, even at this late date, they continued to hold in the highest esteem.

"Then they did not listen," said Lame Dog, sheathing his knife. "We must go from this place, we must find a land. This is no life here. This is death."

White Moccasin knew that what he was hearing was the truth, and it was not the first time he'd heard it. But still he counseled patience, still he told them that the Americans, beside whom they fought, could not mean to treat the Sparrow-hawk the same way they treated the Sioux, the Cheyenne, the Blackfoot. The Great White Father in Washington would not do that. He was their friend.

But if that wasn't enough to stay his war chiefs, he would then resort, as he did this time, to, "My medicine is strong, and it says that the time is not right."

"Your medicine, tobacco-planter, has not been strong enough to make the plants grow." Lame Dog was on the verge, as usual, of outright rebellion.

"That is because the land, like the time, is wrong."

And the fierce look the elderly chief gave Lame Dog peeled away the years and was enough to quell the incipient rebellion. This time.

White Moccasin got to his feet.

Private Rasmussen and Corporal Mulberry saw the old man in baggy clothes come out of the large tipi. Rasmussen thought he looked funny, and smiled.

White Moccasin looked up at that moment and the proud, steady look he gave the two soldiers froze the smile on Rasmussen's face. And it made Corporal Mulberry's heart uncalm.

"These men will never rise again," Mulberry told himself and Rasmussen, quietly, "never fight again."

But he was not certain.

three _____

It was late in the day and the teamsters at the rear table were getting wild. They'd had a long haul that day and felt they deserved to drink all they could hold; they'd earned it. But what their bodies could take, their brains couldn't.

Whitey, the barkeep, eyed them nervously. A drunken teamster on the prowl was about as soothing as a grizzly on the prod. Whitey regretted naming his place Drovers Rest. These dudes belonged down the street at the Crazy Whore Saloon. Break that place up and you couldn't tell the difference. "How 'bout you boys settlin' down to a nice game of cards," he called out. "Got all the chips you can use and all the coffee you can drink. The girls won't be down for a while."

"*Coffee?*" one of the five spat distastefully.

"But cards now," said another, "thet's an idee. Bring them chips over, shorty. We'll have us a game."

There were five teamsters. The table they were at was small for a five-man card game. But it, plus the one several feet away, would do just fine. Except there was a fellow seated there. A man with a swarthy, stony face and long hair, wearing buckskins. No apparent gun. No problem.

"Move it, breed. We need that table."

The "breed" didn't hear them or, if he did, made no show of understanding. He just sat, taking his ease, dead still.

"I said move it, breed, or get moved."

There was still no response and the speaker, florid-faced from booze and sun, gained the other man's table with three swift strides. He lay one hand flat on the table and leaned

19

across it, grabbing the alleged breed's buckskins at the throat with a large, calloused hand.

In the blink of an eye, two things happened. The seated man's feet shot out, kicking the teamster's from under him, and a hunting knife flashed out of nowhere to thud into the teamster's hand, nailing it to the table.

The teamster, on his knees, his free hand loosening its grip on the fellow's buckskins, stared unbelievingly at his bleeding hand, pinned to the table.

For a moment his buddies were frozen with shock. Then they grabbed for their guns. They weren't fast, but they weren't real slow, either. Didn't make sense to pack a gun if you were real slow. Man could get killed that way.

Which is what the still-seated man intended, digging for a gun he had tucked away beneath the buckskin shirt.

First Lieutenant Matt Kincaid, Easy Company's adjutant, had stepped out of the rear door of the Drovers to take a pee. While thus occupied, he'd noticed a familiar figure several buildings distant, similarly occupied. Although, from the way Private Dobbs was crouching, he wasn't really sure what he was doing. Matt buttoned up and strolled toward Dobbs. Windy wouldn't miss him for a while; he could practice tracking roaches across the saloon floor, or identify the odors coming from the teamsters at the next table. A noisy crew, well-oiled before they even reached the Drovers, they'd been settling in as Matt was stepping out.

Dobbs didn't see Matt coming. He was concentrating, his face all screwed up. But his screwing up and hunching and straining sure wasn't producing much, just a thin stream.

Private Dobbs's head suddenly snapped around and, as he recognized Matt, his face reddened more than it was already.

"You're not pregnant, are you, Private? Sure looks like you're birthing."

"Sure to hell wish I was, sir, I sure to hell do."

"Hurts?"

"Comin' out like pure fire, sir."

Matt rarely fooled around in town, and did so only when he could say, *There's a woman like a dewdrop, she's so purer than the purest.*

If Phil Sheridan knew he had an Indian-fighting officer riding around the High Plains quoting Robert Browning, he'd probably shit a brick. But he didn't, and wouldn't. Captain

Warner Conway was the only one who knew, and he was sworn to secrecy.

At the moment, though, laying a hand on poor Stretch Dobbs's shoulder, Matt left aside the poetry and spoke brutally of more mundane matters—namely, they were soldiers, and a man laid up with a red-hot pecker was no help to his comrades. There was only one treatment, a painful treatment, and Matt told him what it was and where to get it done.

"How do *you* know, sir?" asked Dobbs, smiling gamely, trying to establish some kind of rapport.

"And if you don't get it done *now*, immediately, I'll see that you get to hurt even worse."

The six-foot-seven-inch Dobbs was now down to maybe five-ten. He nodded slowly, but then said, "Maybe if I didn't drink nothin' . . ."

Matt's look got harder and Dobbs started nodding again.

Matt left Dobbs leaning against the building with one arm stretched out for support, and walked back to the Drovers.

Coming back through the rear door he heard, "You mangy, bloody breed!" and didn't like the sound of it. His hands were already reaching for his Scoff and his second gun, a Peacemaker, before he actually saw what was happening. As he stepped through the door, his guns came level and fired.

The teamsters' guns hadn't quite cleared leather when the blasts came. Two bottles of whiskey atop their table exploded. They froze.

"Just slide 'em back home easy, boys," said Matt.

Windy Mandalian, chief scout for Easy Company and probably really a breed (rumored to be of Cree descent), slid his Walker Colt back home, too. He'd figured on taking at least two of the bastards with him, as lousy a draw as he was.

The teamsters sobering quickly, realized that they were not only fooling with a fast, dead shot but with the army. With mute anger they awaited instructions.

"You boys better get that hand fixed up," said Matt, "and find somewhere else to drink."

The teamsters shuffled out. One kicked over a table on the way, and another fell over that table. Nothing was going right.

Some time later, after the rubble had been cleared up and Matt had learned what had happened, he asked, "Why the hell didn't you just move?"

"They didn't ask proper. And they didn't give me time."

"Well, hell, at least it's not as boring as it was."

21

"You bored? I'm not. Got me three gals over at the village, two Cheyenne, one Sioux, 'bout as eager as I've ever seen. I'm about as un-bored as I can be, just thinkin' about them."

"Then how come you're here and not there?"

"Can't stand to see a man bored all by himself."

It didn't make sense, but then, it wasn't supposed to. Just Windy's way of saying they were friends.

"You could have been killed," Matt reminded him.

"Got big medicine . . . named Matt." Windy frowned. "But how come you were gone so long? I almost got kilt."

Matt explained about Dobbs, and Windy described an old Indian treatment involving a swift, sharp knife. Matt laughed, shuddered, and retired into his own gloomy thoughts.

He was into his thirties, with a clean record—in war, peace, and bed—but here he was, still a first lieutenant and likely to remain that as long as the rank-freeze held. Washington didn't mind hiring thousands of new recruits and shipping them West—hell, they *had* to, or the voters would get someone who would; the voters weren't about to head West and subdue Mr. Lo—but Washington wasn't ready to pay more to those who were already out there. Probably accounted for a lot of desertions. Fort Keogh had lost damn near a third of its men the past spring. But the weather might have had something to do with that. One Montana winter was about all a Georgia private was going to take.

But it was a consolation that Matt had companions in the same boat, or on the same hobby-horse to nowhere. Easy Company's commander, Captain Warner Conway, hadn't been promoted any more recently than had Matt. And Conway was in his forties and the green grass of retirement wasn't all that far off, but every time Warner Conway thought of having to retire on a captain's pension, well, Matt heard about it, usually through the walls of the officers' quarters.

Easy's other officers, second lieutenants, didn't count. Some were career, some weren't, despite what they all thought at the start, but they usually came and went so fast that Matt had trouble keeping track of what "mister" he was talking to. Mr. Smaldoon, for instance. Up from the ranks, sharp as a tack and a pain in the ass. Matt had called him Smiley, forgetting that Smiley was dead, fallen in a recent Sioux firefight. Smiley'd been up from the ranks, too.

Matt shook his head. Anyone fierce enough to get a battlefield commission, which was what a lot of those up-from-the-

22

ranks men had, was all the more apt to "fierce" himself into an early grave. Maybe he'd mention that to Mr. Smaldoon the next time he had his chin sticking out too far.

Matt's thoughts returned to his own situation. Maybe if he did something unusual, like overpowering the entire Sioux Nation singlehandedly, he'd rate some captain's bars.

"What's so funny?" asked Windy.

"The captain'd probably shoot himself if that happened."

Windy gave him an odd look. "It's gettin' late, Matt. You gonna eat here or get back?"

Mr. Price's wife, Polly, was cooking that night for the officers and their dependents, and she usually burned everything, or left it raw. And Mess Sergeant Dutch Rothausen had the men scheduled, unless he was mistaken, for beans and canned beef. Or, as the men called them, "musical fruit and galvanized cows."

"I think I'll eat here," Matt said.

"There's chili at Elmer's that'll cure whatever you got and give you what you ain't never dreamed of," Windy suggested.

Matt smiled. "That's where I sent Dobbs. I think I'll pass on that."

Not that there was that much to pass on to.

They didn't leave town until nine. There was still a dim half-light hanging over the High Plains as they started, and when that faded, a half-moon took up the slack.

The land was gently rolling, easy to ride even in pitch blackness. The final stretch was slightly uphill, since Outpost Number Nine was located on the most commanding piece of ground the Plains had to offer right around there. Slightly elevated, with a clear view for a few hundred yards in all directions, it was not quite beyond rifle range from the nearest draw, but well out of reach of any arrow.

Nearing the post, Matt and Windy saw light flickering on the flagpole, which was centered in the parade and rose some fifty feet. It looked like the men had a bonfire going, as if the days weren't warm enough.

Riding in through the gate, though, they saw that it wasn't a bonfire. Rather, a large cross had been stuck in the ground in front of the enlisted barracks and set afire.

Matt had seen it before, ten years earlier. He hadn't liked it then and he liked it even less now.

Most of the enlisted men stood outside the barracks, watch-

23

ing. It was too dark to see anyone's face clearly—just forms, shapes. But he recognized Private Enright, moving among the men restlessly, perhaps angrily.

Enright *was* angry. And as he pushed through the men, back and forth, he growled, "If I catch the bastards..." No one needed any further explanations.

Enright was trailed by Weasel Gillies, and Weasel by the kid, Billy.

Gillies hoped Enright would find the men. He wanted action. And justice. Though not for this particular incident. Gillies knew who'd set the cross afire—Popper and Kazmaier—and couldn't care less, but those two rode him as much or more than anyone. They deserved whatever Enright could give them.

Hell, if he had to, he'd tell Enright himself. But Enright probably wouldn't believe him.

Gillies moved carefully. He'd almost been trampled by Enright a few times, on cutbacks, and had taken a lot of random elbows. He finally ducked into the barracks, thinking maybe he'd leave Enright a note. That way, Enright wouldn't know who to disbelieve. He suddenly had to dodge to keep from ramming into Clara Plowright, Sergeant Ernest "Blowhard" Plowright's wife.

Blowhard was the enlistees' name for the bluff, boot-polishing squad leader from Third Platoon. He'd just been made sergeant. He'd probably get transferred out—there wasn't room for him at Easy, unless he wanted to stay a squad leader, normally a corporal's job—and the sooner the better. Gillies had been in his squad for a while, and Blowhard had tried to grind him into the sod. And dammit, he had succeeded too. But Gillies had been ground down before, by meaner, tougher gents than Plowright—his own effin' father, for one—and none had been able to finish the job.

But what the hell had Plowright's wife been doing? Gillies hoped Blowhard wasn't waiting just for him.

"Hey, watch where you're walkin', kid."

"Then don't stop so fast," said Billy.

Gillies advanced cautiously. He looked around. And saw Parker. Parker saw him. Parker sneered. Seems like they all were sneering of late. Give me a gun, thought Gillies, and I'll blow that sneer away. Better yet, give me my old, trusty, two-inch blade. I'd work on that sneer some.

Now he thought: Plowright and Parker? Why not? Clara

always looked hotter than a pistol. And he'd bet Blowhard Plowright packed nothing better than a popgun. That was likely what made him so mean.

Gillies looked around some more. So did Billy.

Damn, thought Gillies, these dudes just leave everything right out where you can grab it.

Outside the barracks, Captain Conway and Master Sergeant Ben Cohen bore down on the flaming cross and the crowd around it. No one had thought to douse the flames.

Actually, Matt Kincaid had, but he preferred to let it burn while he studied faces. He didn't like some looks he saw. Popper's, for one. And Private Barrett, standing back against the barracks wall, looked as though he were about to have a heart attack.

"Get this fire out," spat Captain Conway, now on the scene, and twenty men jumped.

Pails flew from the mess, and the blaze was soon an ember. But the fire was still in Captain Conway's eyes. "Who did this?" he demanded, quietly but distinctly.

No one spoke, or even blinked. It sure sounded like the Captain's "hanging voice."

"I would like to know who is responsible for this," said Captain Conway, "and why. But I don't suppose I will." His lips creased briefly into a cold smile.

"Now," he said, "I don't condone barracks justice. Why, I don't know anything about it; I've never heard of such a thing." He shook his head slowly, as if saddened by revelations of the depths to which men might sink.

"In any case," he said, brightening, "Sergeant Cohen will have you men falling out an hour early tomorrow morning. And I think that will become the routine, until I see fit to stop it." This time it was a warm smile. "Do we understand each other?"

And he turned on his heel and walked off. Not toward his quarters, but rather toward the orderly room. Matt, Sergeant Cohen, and the three junior officers took their cue from him and also walked in that direction.

They hadn't gone far when they heard a shout from the barracks. "Hey! Somebody's stole my watch!"

As a group, the officers hesitated, but Ben Cohen kept right on going and then they did too.

25

four ───────────

They gathered in the orderly room. Captain Conway visited his own office briefly, to tidy his uniform, and Matt Kincaid ducked into his to get a bottle of rye.

"Didn't have to do that, sir," said Cohen. "I could've done the honors."

"Why don't we save yours for real honors, then. This is different. I was stationed in North Carolina the last time I saw one of those crosses."

"What was it?" asked Lieutenant Price, platoon leader of First Platoon, and all eyes turned his way. "I mean, it did seem rather irreligious. . . ." His voice trailed off.

"A burning cross is the symbol of the Klan, Mr. Price. You have heard of the Klan, haven't you?"

Mr. Price nodded, and Matt Kincaid smiled. Price was probably hopeless. He was naive and uninformed, but good-hearted. Price fancied himself an expert in the art of fisticuffs, but he was no fighter. Fortunately, First Platoon had Sergeant Gus Olsen for platoon sergeant, and Matt himself generally rode with the First, so any damage Price might do was mini-mized.

"I rode with the Klan once," said Mr. Smaldoon, and the looks he got made him immediately regret his words. "Before I was with the army, mind you."

"Perhaps you didn't recall that Mr. Lincoln was *your* Pres-ident, too," said Captain Conway menacingly, "whether you liked it or not. The Ninth and Tenth Cav are black, and if they're good enough to be soldiers, they're good enough not to get goddamn crosses burned in front of their homes. Where are you from, Mr. Smaldoon?"

26

"Maine."

"Maine? The Klan's in *Maine?*"

"Family moved South, sir. I never seen a nigger till I was seventeen."

"Try 'colored,'" suggested Conway.

"Try what?"

"'Colored,' instead of 'nigger' . . . or if you're really ambitious, say Negro."

Conway was going to let it go at that. But Smaldoon, trying to ease the situation, trying to laugh it off, smiled winningly and asked, "Is that an order, sir?" He thought he'd made a joke.

Conway's eyes hardened. "Yes, goddammit, it is."

Mr. Allison, West Pointer from Virginia, platoon leader for the Third, and that day's OD, said, "Assuming the cross meant what we think it means, who the hell have we got that's Negro? Or part Negro, as is undoubtedly the case?"

"I would guess," said Matt, "that just a few know who it is, or who they *think* it is. Most of the men looked puzzled as hell, like Mr. Price here." He grinned. "But we might question Enright. He not only looked like he might know who the colored man is, but was damn pissed that someone did this."

"Mr. Allison," said Captain Conway, "get Enright here. Then get the guard sergeant—who is it, Chubb?—get him and the corporal here."

"I don't think I know Enright, sir."

"Just walk over to the barracks, Bob," said Matt Kincaid. "Step inside, and after they've come to attention you say, 'Private Enright, follow me,' and then you walk out. I guarantee you'll get your man."

Allison had started nodding halfway through, and he looked properly chastened. "Not always that dumb," he muttered as he headed for the door.

Ten minutes later, Enright was standing in front of Sergeant Cohen's desk, not a little cowed by the amount of brass assembled. It felt like a court-martial.

"What do you know about what happened over there, Enright?" asked Sergeant Cohen, glaring.

"Nothing, Sarge. Like to catch the bastards that did it, though."

"Why?"

"'Cause I figure it was thinking like that that almost got my ass shot off in the War."

"The Klan came *after* the War, Private," said Smaldoon.

Enright eyed Smaldoon carefully. "Begging your pardon, sir, and I may be wrong, but I said it was *thinking* like that, and I still think the thinking's the same." Enright was neither foolish nor fearless, but on some things he was a little stubborn, no matter what the consequences.

"Well, Private, you're wrong," declared Smaldoon.

"No, you're *not* wrong," contradicted Captain Conway, "Mr. Smaldoon's wrong."

Smaldoon's eyes widened. He liked the captain, but it seemed Conway was about to commit a reportable breach of military etiquette, if not regulations, and over a *nigger*, to boot. Smaldoon hadn't fought his way up to sit quietly for something like that.

Matt Kincaid and Sergeant Cohen started shouting before Conway could get his mouth open again. Matt demanded the bottle of rye and Cohen roared, "Where the hell are Chubb and Plowright, goddammit?" Even Enright got into the act, asserting, "But there's something else, sir, that may be just as important." Enright's capacity for sympathy, like his sense of justice and his love for a good fight, could sometimes be extraordinary.

Just then, Sergeants Chubb and Plowright entered.

"Dammit, Chubb, where've you been?" roared Captain Conway.

Chubb blinked for a few seconds, then said, "Gol-lee, Captain, I just got through fightin' off a whole mess of renegade Cheyenne. Got here soon's I could."

Conway blinked himself. Sergeant Chubb had literally saved Conway's scalp in the recent past and had never mentioned the fact to a soul. Actually, Conway was lucky Sergeant Breckenridge wasn't sergeant of the guard. Breckenridge would just have stared him down, spat on the floor, turned, and walked out. Top noncoms weren't that easy to come by, and the noncoms knew it.

Conway's eyes made his apology even while he was saying, "Don't get smart, Sergeant, I'm not in the mood. Now, do any of your men know anything about that fire?"

"I asked 'em, sir. If they know anythin', they ain't sayin'."

"How about you, Plowright?"

"What fire, sir?"

28

"He was sleepin', sir," explained Sergeant Chubb. "Sergeant Plowright's so pissed at having to pull corporal of the guard that he felt he had to sleep it off. I told him he deserved a transfer ay-propriate to his elevation in rank, and that I heard Colonel Miles was about to send a detachment out with orders to kill Crazy Horse or die tryin', and they happened to have room for a kill-crazy sergeant. . . ."

Captain Conway's face had gone slack during Chubb's recital, and now he curtly dismissed Chubb and Plowright.

Then Conway turned to face Enright. "What were you saying about something else, Private?"

"Stuff's missing in the barracks, sir," answered Enright promptly. "We got us a barracks thief."

Conway said, frowning, "This is your area, Sergeant."

Cohen nodded, then asked, "Now what's this?"

"Stuff's missing in the barracks, Sarge. We got—"

"Dammit, I'm not deaf, I heard you before. Who is it?"

"Don't know."

"Find out. Then bring me what's left."

"Some of the men think it's Gillies—or the kid—or both."

"What do you think?"

"Don't know. Never met anyone like them. Seems they grow them different in the city. Small, tough, and maybe mean. 'Cept the kid's the same way, and he's from out here. He's taken a shine to Gillies."

"Weasel . . . Weasel's like a rat, ain't it?"

"Guess so, Sarge. I call him Gillies."

"Yeah. You do, but the rest don't. Maybe the rest are right for a change. What do you think of that?"

Enright didn't say. Cohen waved a hand in dismissal. "Right. You men find out, let me know. And go get some sleep. You're gettin' up early tomorrow, unless you'd care to let us know who did the burning."

"If I knew, they'd be lying outside your door, Sergeant," said Enright, and he turned and walked out.

"Where'd that bottle go?" Cohen wanted to know.

Matt handed him the bottle, but his attention was elsewhere. Captain Conway's face was unusually drawn. "What's the matter, Captain?"

Conway stared at Matt. "I'm just not looking forward to the moment I learn that there *is* a man in this company who's part Negro . . . and who that man is." Conway's face broke into a wry smile; he'd been in situations a hell of a lot more hairy

29

than the one he was anticipating. "Hell, Matt, look around. Do you see anyone that *looks* Negro? But we all know what policy is. It doesn't matter what my personal opinion might be, or yours. If a man is legally a Negro, even if he's lily-white, he either belongs with the colored troops or he doesn't belong at all—that's policy."

"You don't like it, sir?" inquired Mr. Smaldoon.

Captain Conway eyed him coldly. "I have no opinion, Mr. Smaldoon. There is policy and there are orders, nothing else." He turned away from Smaldoon. "But Matt, do you remember when they were trying to decide, legally, just what constituted a colored man?"

Matt laughed. "Yeah. First the states said that if a man was only one-quarter colored, he could call himself a white man, legally, and then they found they had all these obviously black men that could prove themselves white."

"So then," completed Conway, "they changed it to one-eighth—or was it one-sixteenth?—just to be certain."

"I wonder what it is for the Indian?" said Mr. Allison. "What percentage?"

"Don't know if it was ever decided," said Captain Conway. "Don't know if anyone ever cared. The Indians were never slaves."

"There's not a hell of a lot of difference now, though," said Matt, showing he knew what Allison was talking about.

Some time later, Matt Kincaid was on his way toward his quarters when he encountered Clara Plowright.

"Howdy, Mrs. Plowright," he said, fingering the brim of his forage cap even though the night was pitch black; the early moon was gone. "That's a might attractive perfume you're wearing." Powerful and penetrating, too—she was inclined to overdo it.

"The shape tells me it's a tall, broad-shouldered man and the voice that it's handsome Lieutenant Matt Kincaid."

"That's a real mouthful, ma'am, that I'm sure I don't deserve."

"What *do* you deserve, Lieutenant?"

Matt was busy being polite and had trouble turning that one over in his mind. "Ummmm, well, I reckon what everybody needs right now is a good night's rest."

"Rest?" she echoed, chuckling.

"Sure feel sorry for your husband, ma'am, stuck out on guard all night."

"He'll survive. He's probably sleeping."

"So I understand."

"He's very good at sleeping. Are you any good? At sleeping?"

"Like the dead."

"I'll bet."

He sensed her smile in the darkness. "Which reminds me," he said, "I'm half-dead already, so I'll have to be saying good night, and it was sure a pleasure running into you like this." He edged past her and backed away. "And I sure hope you get a good night's rest yourself."

Her low, gurgling laugh followed him.

In his quarters he discovered that the kerchief around his neck had gotten damned tight.

In town, several men gathered in a saloon.

"Y'bring yer sheet west with yuh, Harvey?"

Harvey glared at the speaker. He might well have been accused of wearing pajamas.

"Yer *Klan* sheet, dummy!"

"What fer? Ain't no niggers aroun' here."

"They's Injuns. They're gittin' t' be near as bad. They're gittin' to thinkin' they're *white*."

"Wal, they *is* whiter than niggers."

"They still ain't white. Yestiddy I actual had to wait in line b'hind a Injun, down to the feed store. Bastard was buyin' *seed*. Whaddaya think *that* means?"

"They're gonna plant somethin'?"

"They're fixin' to *stay*. They're aimin' to settle in and pretty soon them damn little brown kids'll be all over the place, stinkin'. An' you know how they stink."

"You don' smell lahk no dream y'self, Kurt."

"Nothin' lahk them, buddy. An' ah seen somethin' else. One of them squaws, she had her tit out, right there in public, stretchin' down about t' her waist! We got our womenfolk to think about, our *kids*. We can't let them git exposed to all thet Injun immorality, now kin we?"

A chorus of denials.

"We oughta go shoot 'em up, send 'em packin'."

"Cain't do that, 'lessen we kin git them t' shoot first. The

31

army's right picky about thet."

"Th' *army!* Bunch of old ladies."

"I saw a breed git a whole buncha white men, teamsters got 'em all shot up down t' the Drovers a while back."

"Kilt?"

"Noooo. Sure scared, though. But the feller what did the actual shootin' was a army gent. Some officer."

"Kincaid?"

"Don' know."

"Prob'ly was. Got him a pearl-handled job?" A nod. "Yeah. Effin' Kincaid. Hear he's near an Injun-lover hisself. Breed was prob'ly the scout. Them two is tight . . . if you know what I mean."

The man was willing to say or suggest anything to rally support.

"But you just wait, and be ready. Them Injuns is bound to do *somethin'*. Then we'll land on 'em.

Enright went looking for Jeff Barrett. He found him sitting crosslegged near the center of the parade.

"What are you doing?"

"Meditating."

"Hm?"

"Waiting for a dream, a vision." Barrett knew Indians did it; why couldn't he?

"Come on in and meditate in the sack."

"I'm not going in there anymore."

"Oh."

Enright didn't feel like arguing. It was late. He turned and walked back to the barracks.

five _____

"Where are the horses, White Moccasin? Without horses, we Sparrowhawk are nothing. You said when the agency took our horses they promised to give us more."

White Moccasin looked down at his baggy trousers. Indeed they had. And they had not done as they had promised. In his heart he'd known that they would not, that they did not want the Sparrowhawk on horses.

His eyes rose to meet those of Lame Dog. "Why do we need horses, Lame Dog? We are going nowhere."

"But who are we without horses? My father owned more than sixty horses. And in battle it was I who drew first blood from the enemy. So when my father gave away all his possessions, for being the father of the first to cut in battle, he was rich and had many horses to give...." Lame Dog smiled sadly. "Do you remember how many times I made him give all away? My success in battle nearly ruined my poor father."

"I do remember. And I was among those who then shared their wealth with your father so that he might be rich again and have more to give away when next you triumphed. We were all proud of you. My own son was a brave warrior too, but he was also proud of you and he gave many of his possessions to your father."

"I do remember, White Moccasin. Perhaps I should say nothing. But if *my* son, when of age, should draw first blood, I will have nothing to give away. No horses, no robes so beautifully stitched by my wives, no trophies..."

"I cry for you, Lame Dog, and whatever I have is yours,

33

but your son will not draw first blood, will not be the first to cut. We will be fighting no more. We have given our word."

Lame Dog drew himself up proudly. "And what word has the American given?" He made the sign of the forked tongue, spat on the ground, and walked off.

White Moccasin caught hold of his trousers as they were about to slide down his legs, and tied the rope belt tight again.

He looked about, then up at the sky. It was a beautiful day, up *there*.

He was hungry, but there was little to eat. The day before, the agent had made him a great present, very unusual. He had given him, Chief White Moccasin, chief among the Sparrowhawk, among the mountain Absaroka, the fresh killed carcass of a bull cow. It had been salted (an unusual taste for a Crow) and was meant to last the chief for many moons. But according to the Sparrowhawk custom, when one is rich, then all are rich, and he had shared his meat with the village and it had lasted for less than two hours.

Nor was there milk. They had gone away to visit and the milk cow had dried up. He did not understand such things. He was supposed to plant crops and live on milk and leaves and grain and berries, he who had never lived on anything but meat—meat of the buffalo, meat of the antelope.

He was hungry.

He wanted to hunt.

Jeff Barrett had gone to town. While pulling KP, he'd overheard Sergeant Rothausen yearn for a spice that Dutch thought could be bought in town. Barrett had immediately volunteered to race to town and pick some up.

He stood in line at the general store. He should have felt tired. He'd stayed up the entire night, trying to produce a dream, a vision, and then had gone straight to KP. But he wasn't tired. And he didn't plan to be tired, nor did he plan to rest, until he'd seen his vision.

Of course, maybe he'd seen it already, in 1866. It had certainly preoccupied him over the years, driven him to study the language. But what role was there for a Mountain Man, much less a Crow chief, to play these days?

"Least we don't hafta wait b'hind no Injuns today."

"I ain't never gonna wait behind no Injun agin."

Barrett's head turned. Three of the men that had gathered

and complained in the saloon the previous evening were standing there. They were broad men of average height, hard-muscled and knobby-browed.

Barrett said, "You're waiting behind one now."

The men looked around the store, puzzled. They didn't see any Indians, and the man ahead of Barrett at the counter was so German you could hardly understand him.

"What the hell you talkin' about, blue-leg? Marchin' aroun' in the hot sun musta got to yer haid."

"I'm part Indian," said Barrett. "Can't you tell? I'm taller than you, stronger than you. Better looking than you, what else could I be?" He grinned. "And I'm standing in front of you dummies and you're just gonna have to wait until I get through my ordering. Might take some time, too."

Unfortunately, Barrett wasn't bigger and stronger than all three. They took his size into account, added the army uniform, noted the absence of any obvious army backup, and after totaling up all those considerations . . . they started swinging.

Barrett had a moment to realize that in his weariness he'd miscalculated the depth of their hostility. After that he was fighting for his life, or his limbs, anyway.

The first blows backed him up, squashing the German into the counter. They landed on his shoulders and high on his ribcage. Roundhouse swings, but with plenty of weight and passion.

He snapped out some lightning jabs, but he might as well have been punching boulders. One man he could have taken easily, two with difficulty, but three? Not when they were coming at him simultaneously from three different directions.

He decided to concentrate on the most offensive speaker, the one on his right. He drove fist after fist into the man's hard face, closing an eye, flattening a nose. . . .

But his blows got weaker. He began to pull them, tucking in his elbows to protect his torso, which, along with his arms and shoulders, was almost numb. He could barely keep his fists raised. His body began to curl up, the organism closing in on itself defensively.

He lost track of time and no longer had any sense of injury. And before he lost consciousness he heard triumphant epithets and the sound of spitting. He was grateful when the blackness came. . . .

During which blackness he finally had his vision, of leading

35

the resurgent red man against the white man, of destroying the rapacious Americans.

The Bloody Arm of the Great Spirit . . .

He also suffered a concussion that carried with it the possibility of slight brain damage; the boys had done a real job on him. Whether or not this affected his subsequent behavior is impossible to say.

He came to with the storekeeper crouched over him. His face and shoulders were wet, his clothing soaked. A bucket was by his head, a wet rag draped over the rim.

He tried moving. He ached some, and would ache a hell of a lot more later, he knew, but nothing was broken. He got to his feet.

His face was cut and bruised, but the bleeding had stopped. Jesus, how long had he been out?

"'Bout fifteen minutes, I reckon," said the storekeeper.

Barrett staggered off to sit on an upended barrel. The storekeeper brought him a cup of water and a hunk of bread. Barrett took them and then sat for a long while gathering his strength, his wits, and pulling his dream, his *vision*, out for a good looksee.

Several customers came and went, the women eyeing him with concern, the men with wonder, or, having heard about the fight, with open amusement . . . until he looked up and caught their eye.

At length, the store empty, Barrett got to his feet and went to the counter.

"You ain't really Injun, is you, son?" He took Barrett's vague smile for denial. He checked the store once more for emptiness. "I kin tell you where thet trash hangs out, iffen you want."

Barrett did want, and the man told him.

Barrett then ordered the spice he'd ridden in to get. "And then let me have some dried beef, some coffee, some biscuits, stuff for the trail, you'll know what I want."

The storekeeper wondered, but didn't question. He suspected, though, that the three Indian-haters might have some trouble heading their way.

Barrett went from the general store to the livery. "Like to borrow a horse," he told the hostler. He smiled inwardly. When

36

the Crow stole a horse, they thought of it as borrowing. They had no sense of personal property when it came to horses, especially Sioux or Blackfoot horses. Horses were practically legal (or illegal) tender to them.

"Yers lame?"

"Nope. Got a friend."

"Two bits a day. That's with a saddle."

"Not a McClellan, is it?"

"Hell, no."

Good. Might save his testicles a little wear and tear. The army liked McClellans. Horses liked McClellans. Riders didn't.

And so Private Barrett rode from town carrying his bag of spice and leading a horse loaded down with gear.

He tied the horse up in a cottonwood-thick draw about a mile from Outpost Number Nine and hoped no predator, human or otherwise, happened by. Then he rode to the post, where he resumed his KP duties.

That night, finished with KP, Barrett headed for the day room to await taps and full darkness. He thought the day room might be empty—reading was not a popular diversion and the men generally preferred to have their card games in the barracks or outside—but he was wrong. The place was packed. The wives on post had chosen that night to entertain the boys with cards and games and friendly female companionship. A little bit of gentility couldn't hurt men whose lives were so unremittingly dreary.

Actually, the idea had come from Flora Conway, the captain's better and prettier half. Flora was blond, beautiful, and, though in her thirties, still luscious, possibly because she was childless. And being childless, it was not surprising that she'd chosen to adopt the men and boys of Easy Company as her own. To Flora they were all "dear," and nothing was too good for them. That sometimes made it tough for Captain Conway to enforce discipline, and might prompt her to keep to her own side of the bed for several nights, actively discouraging visitation. But the freeze never lasted for long. Healthy lust, for which this Virginia-bred and properly raised woman had never found a name, always made its presence known, sooner or later.

So the entertainment for the men had been Flora's idea, one

37

the other wives had welcomed or been afraid to resist. There
was Jennifer Allison, as demure as Flora Conway had once
been (and still was, in Warner Conway's eyes); Polly Price,
whose recent arrival kept Mr. Price from climbing the flagpole
(as the men liked to joke); Cassie Smaldoon, Mr. Smaldoon's
sister, of all things, come West to catch a man of respectable
rank; Clara Plowright, already married but not acting like it;
Amy Breckenridge, who looked like a draft animal the sergeant
should have left back in Tennessee with his in-laws, who played
ferocious poker and could outwrestle half the men in Easy.
Breckenridge obviously needed every ounce of taciturnity he
owned.

Then there was Maggie Cohen, Ben's wife. Easy Company
was Maggie's "family" too, but her family had a star member:
Flora Conway. What Flora could do and did for others, she
couldn't do for herself. So Maggie did it. If Flora was Easy's
mother, then Maggie was its grandmother. She was younger
than Flora, though, and heavier, but she had a nice sense of
humor.

It was not with despair that Private Barrett regarded the
assemblage. The women's presence assured his being left
alone, made certain that no ill-chosen words would be bandied
about. Barrett sat in for a hand of poker with Amy Breckenridge, getting a close look at her forearms and wishing he'd
had her fighting alongside him back in town. She smiled as
she gathered in the few coins he risked, and seemed sorry to
see him retire to a corner of the room.

Barrett took out a pipe, a slender thing gracefully carved
and decorated with quiet colors and a few beads—his calumet,
he called it—and then sat in the corner, smoking, relaxing,
again thinking of his vision.

He supposed he should thank his assailants.

Well, in a way he thought he might just do that.

A throbbing began in his head, and there was a burst of
pain . . . but then it went away.

Some time later a soldier entered the day room and said quietly
but forcefully and clearly, "There's been another stealin', and
it's gonna be the last."

A number of eyes sought out Weasel Gillies.

Weasel smiled down at his cards, oblivious to the stares.
He'd seen Clara Plowright slip out and then back in. He'd

figured she was rendezvousing with Parker, but maybe she wasn't.

"You gents oughtn't to leave yer stuff out like that," he said, without looking up. "Jes' askin' fer trouble, an' y'all deserve all y' get—or all the thief gets." And then he looked up.

His eyes narrowed. He didn't know fear. But he knew danger.

six _____

The next morning, reveille, grub call and then assembly came at their usual times. But just by a hair.

The bugler, Reb McBride, had hauled himself from the sack an hour early and was trying to adjust his lips to the cold brass when a shout came from the orderly room.

Sergeant Cohen, in his skivvies, was out front looking down at Kazmaier and Popper, who were just then coming around. They'd had a note pinned to them, which Cohen had already detached and read.

"Got us our cross-burners, Corp," Cohen told McBride. "You go get yourself another hour's sleep."

Reb, who, as a kid, had blown the charge for many a crack Southern outfit, stomped off toward Dutch's mess, wondering how in the world the South could've lost to a misbegotten bunch of sleep-robbing clowns such as these. He said as much to the gummy-eyed Dutch, and then, sipping coffee, answered himself:

"Any army that can live on this coffee and your grub can lick *anybody*."

With a slight change in emphasis, it could have been a compliment. "Hope you were meanin' that in a nice way," said Dutch.

"You study cookin' at Penn State?" Most of the men knew that Dutch had gone to Penn State. But to such an ill-educated bunch, going to Penn State was like going to England or France. And Reb was no exception.

"Nope, somethin' better." He gathered in his ample belly with both arms. "I studied *eatin'*."

An hour later came reveille, and an hour after that came assembly. Normally, assembly was a fast round of all-present-and-accounted-fors, followed by a brief assigning of duties and details prior to dismissal. Not this time, though.

First and Second Platoons were fine, but . . .

"Third Pluh-*toon* has *foh*-uhh men missing. Thuh-*reee* is ay-counted foh-uh and one is *un*-ay-counted for-uh."

Mr. Allison was standing with the other junior officers in a line behind Captain Conway and Lieutenant Kincaid. His eyes closed slowly and he sighed.

Cohen couldn't help smiling. Sergeant Chubb seemed to find something to enjoy in any and every situation, no matter how difficult or unpleasant. "Kazmaier and Popper I know about," said Cohen. "They're tucked away safe in the guardhouse. Cross-burners."

"Guardhouse, y' say," commented Chubb. "My, my. I thought they were still heaped up in a corner of the barracks."

"Who else?"

"Private John Gillies, more affectionately known as Weasel. He's inside, tryin' to die. Don't think he's gonna make it, though. Tough little hombre."

"Right, wrap him up and bring him to me, we'll see what's going on, though I got an idea. And the last?"

"Private Barrett," drawled Chubb. "Ain't been seen since last night in the day room."

"Have your men take a look around, Sergeant, just in case," Cohen said, adding a low, heartfelt, "goddammit."

"Easy there, Sergeant," came Conway's equally low voice from behind.

Of course, behind *that* there came, lower still, "I'd kill the bastard, Bob." Smaldoon, a real sweetheart, giving Bob Allison advice.

Cohen pivoted around, threw a salute up at Captain Conway, and said, "Easy Company, four men missing, three accounted for, one . . . one still to be found."

Captain Conway returned the salute. "Take care of it, Sergeant," he said, then turned and strolled toward the officers' mess.

Smaldoon, Price, and Allison fell in behind the captain.

41

Matt Kincaid matched Cohen stride for stride back to the orderly room.

"What do you think, Sergeant?"

"Got an idea that Weasel's the thief, or at least that's what the men beat him up for.... Got Kazmaier and Popper dumped on me this morning, courtesy of Enright."

Kincaid's eyebrows rose. "Enright?"

"Enright. He's a bloody terror when he wants to be, and he usually wants to be when it's a matter of right and wrong. Damn, he'd make a good Jew. They'd call him Moses."

Kincaid grinned, and Cohen went on, "Anyway, Kazmaier and Popper were the cross-burners. But Barrett? What was it Windy said, that he didn't think Barrett was part Indian? Well, he ain't. He's the colored man the cross-burning was about. Bein' found out must have turned his head around. And Maggie saw him last night, said he looked beat up. You hear anything about that?"

"A while ago, Dutch said the same. Said Barrett went to town yesterday to pick up something for him, came back a mess, but wouldn't talk about it."

"Huh. Well, maybe he's just hid out someplace, curled up in the sutler's, maybe, or the stables. Never had time to figure Barrett out, but I thought he seemed a little peculiar at times."

"Your imagination. Seemed okay to me."

"I ain't got any imagination, Matt, you know that. And he looked up to you."

"Looked up to you too, Sergeant."

Cohen didn't argue, but instead only mused, "Him and Weasel both came in about the same time. Some package..."

A half-hour later, Sergeant Chubb, trailed by Sergeant Breckenridge, showed up in the orderly room to report that Barrett was nowhere on post... unless he was hidden in someone's quarters where he oughtn't have been.

"There ain't no horses missing," Chubb volunteered. "Don't figger he could've walked too far."

Matt Kincaid stared at him. "Maybe it wasn't anything sudden. Maybe it was planned. And he did go to town yesterday...."

"Let me take a patrol out," suggested Breckenridge. "Scout around, look for some kinda horse tetherin'..."

"Go," said Ben Cohen, and Breckenridge ambled off.

Chubb also left, and five minutes later was back with John

"Weasel" Gillies in tow. "The men say he's been thievin' them blind. *He* says they deserve to be thieved—"

"He didn't steal nothin'!" came a cry from the doorway, and Ben and Matt caught a glimpse of little Billy before he ducked out of sight.

Chubb didn't need to see Billy. "The men also think Gillies here might have had a confederate, even littler'n him."

Sergeant Cohen and Matt Kincaid stared at Gillies; he wasn't pretty under normal circumstances, and now his natural ugliness was augmented by numerous gashes, bruises, and welts.

"Appears a powerful lot of fightin' went on in the barracks last night," Chubb said. "A wonder they had any time to sleep. Enright don't have a scratch on him, though. Deals himself out some mighty hard justice, he does."

"What would you have done?" Kincaid asked.

"Prob'ly strung 'em up real quiet," Chubb replied. "As for Gillies here, the men that did it to him didn't exactly get off scot-free. Our friend here has a couple of fast feet and sharp toes. Ol' Parker just about had to crawl to assembly."

"Parker's messin' with Miz Plowright," Weasel yelped, and all three men turned and stared at him.

"You'd best shut up about stuff like that," Cohen warned him, then added, "how about it, Weasel? The stealin', that is."

Weasel regarded them all sullenly. "The name's Gillies," he said. "*Private* Gillies."

At that moment, both Cohen and Kincaid had about the same thought: that for all his lousy, deprived upbringing—or perhaps because of it—the army was apparently important to this man. As a private in that army he had an identity and some claim to dignity. Not much, certainly, but some, and he seemed willing to fight for it.

"They just leave things around, right out in the open," said Gillies. "They deserve to lose it all, the bastards."

"So you figure if a person gets robbed, he only has himself to blame," suggested Matt. "That he shouldn't have been where he was in the first place, or that he should have kept his stuff locked up, and that's the way it was where you grew up."

"Yeah," said Gillies, almost defiantly.

"Did you steal the stuff?" asked Cohen.

"No," Gillies replied just as defiantly as before.

"Why not?"

Gillies took a while to answer. "'Cause this ain't back home, that's why. It's different here...or it's supposed to be...but it ain't, is it?"

"Gillies," said Matt. "That's not Armenian, or whatever you call yourself. Where'd you get it?"

"I took it. When I joined. Ain't nothin' wrong with that."

"Didn't say there was. Who from?"

"Who from what?"

"Who'd you get the name from?"

"Cop on the beat, that's who," said Gillies, not backing off an inch. "An' he kin have it back, all the good it's done me."

Cohen spoke to Chubb. "The men show any proof?"

"Nope. And they would have, if they had any."

"So? What do *you* think?"

"The men ain't liked him since he got here, 'cause he's so runty and different, 'cause he stands up to them all the same, and 'cause he looks like a rat...."

Gillies stiffened.

"Hey, son," said Chubb, "that ain't my fault, or your fault, but you do. It's God's fault. Not a *bad*-lookin' rat, though, I'll give y' that. But anyway, Gillies here knew what they thought of him, and that they'd be waitin' for him to do somethin', and a feller'd have to be pretty stupid to march right into that. And Private Gillies is not stupid, Sarge. Don't know beans, but he ain't stupid."

Gillies looked at him with something like gratitude.

"Phil Sheridan's not very big," muttered Matt.

Cohen grinned briefly. "But he *does* know beans." He looked from Gillies to Chubb. "Take Gillies on back, Sergeant. Let him get some rest. Then find yourself the men that beat him up—they should be taking bows right and left—and find out if they got any evidence. If they *do*, bring it to me. But if they don't, you kick their asses until I say stop. And you tell them that if they ever do come up with any evidence, against *anybody*, they better bring it to me first."

"Right, Sarge. You go along, Gillies, wait outside for me."

Gillies left, and Sergeant Chubb said, "You know it won't change anything, Sarge. They'll still deal out their own justice."

"Yeah, I know, but it's gonna make 'em think, though. And the next time maybe they'll be *right*."

Matt stepped outside to watch Chubb and Weasel make their way back toward the barracks.

This was all happening because the men weren't *doing* anything, thought Matt. What Easy needed was some action, something to keep everybody happy.

He felt a nudge, looked down, and saw Clara Plowright by his side. Good-looking as she was, he still felt himself go cold.

"Awful, isn't it?" she said. "How does the army let a man like that in? Not only is he ugly, but he's a sneak thief too."

"Nothing's been proved, and he probably isn't a thief. He may be ugly, but that depends on who's doing th' looking."

"With some men, it doesn't depend on who's looking."

Matt didn't like the sound of that. "Sergeant Plowright back on guard again?"

"Again? He just got off. He's *sleeping*," she said disgustedly. "You know he was living with two aunts when we met?"

"So? What's wrong with that?"

"He was *thirty-one*."

"He's that old? How long ago was that?" Matt asked.

"Few years."

"Well, all it indicates is that he's a strong family-type man. That should be good."

"Sure, if he only knew how to *make* a family."

"How's that?"

"I only meant that he was very quiet. Very private. Very . . . shy?" She looked up meaningfully at Matt, who began to get the picture.

Later that afternoon, a man rode onto post from town. He represented the law.

Matt and Captain Conway joined Ben Cohen in front of the orderly room, where they looked up at the rider.

"You folks hear of any Indian action hereabouts?"

"Nope," said Sergeant Cohen.

"Wish we had," said Matt, grinning.

"Well," said the law sourly, eyeing Matt, "you got your wish. We got some in town."

"How's that?"

"Found three men this morning, out back of Gert's Watering Hole. Knifed to beat hell. Scalped. Musta happened sometime late last night. No one *seed* it happen, though. Didn't *hear* nothin', neither. . . ."

Ben Cohen looked at Matt and Captain Conway, who were equally speechless.

"Didn't think Indians attacked at night," said the law.

45

"You don't believe that, do you?" Cohen asked.

"Naw. My folks got killed at night. Scalped. But that's what a lot of folks claim."

Matt decided that this representative of the law was not terribly bright, preferring to credit what people said rather than what he knew. "Who got killed?"

"Fellers that worked aroun' town, odd jobs, ranch work sometimes, drank mostly, always wanted to vigilante after someone. If they was alive now, *they'd* be the ones hot to ride off an' kill some Injuns. Funny, ain't it?"

"Can't argue that."

"Hear tell, too, they were fightin' some soldier in the general store yestiddy, beat 'im up."

Matt and Ben Cohen froze, as Captain Conway's expression showed that he didn't believe any man under his command could have been beaten up in town.

"You know anything about that?" asked the law.

"Sounds like nonsense to me," said Warner Conway. He turned to the other two men. "Doesn't it to you?"

"Nonsense," said Ben Cohen.

"Poppycock," said Matt, and Warner Conway's eyes bulged.

"What do you want us to do?" asked Ben.

"Nothin'. Don't figger they's any connection between the beatin' and the killin'. We kin take care of town. Jes' figgered you'd like to know if you was about to have an Indian uprising."

"We certainly would like to know. Thank you. We appreciate it," Conway told the law, who turned his horse and rode on out of the post, heading back to town.

Conway turned to Matt and said, in his fruitiest voice, "Poppycock?"

"Thought I'd tip you off, put you on your guard. Barrett got beat up in town yesterday. Barrett's still missing. He fancied calling himself an Indian."

Captain Conway's face fell. "Oh, shit," he said.

"But look at it this way, sir," said Matt. "With Barrett gone, you don't have the problem of a colored man messing up a U.S. Army company of white men. Gets you off the hook. And if he killed those men, he won't be coming back."

"That's true enough, I suppose." Conway smiled grimly.

seven _____

Barrett had found the three men in Gert's Watering Hole. He was no longer in uniform, and Gert's was dark, so he was unrecognized. He waited in the alley beside the saloon. The three men staggered out well after midnight.

They were almost too drunk to understand the meaning of the guns he pointed at them. Both guns, incidentally, were Scoffs, but not his army guns. The same model, but these had five-inch barrels and had "Wells Fargo," as well as "U.S.," stamped on the side of those barrels. He'd bought them at the general store, choosing them over some '69 S&Ws because, unlike the .44-caliber '69s, they were chambered for .45s. He'd decided that, if nothing else, he'd take the army's ammunition with him.

He'd herded the three drunks down the alley to the rear of Gert's, where he killed them, knifing them deliberately and extensively. It was easy. Lifting the scalps, though, wasn't.

He'd read that it was easiest to collect a scalp when the victim was fresh-killed, if killed at all. But after a sweaty few minutes with the first one, beginning to panic for fear of being discovered, he'd decided that there was a bit more to it than that. The first scalp finally came off, but damn near in shreds. The next two were easier, though. Just needed practice, he decided.

He wrapped the messy things in cloth, tucked them away in a saddlebag, and then rode off. He rode north. There was already a sliver of light on the eastern horizon.

Had it taken him that long? He wished he'd thought to buy a pocket watch.

It wasn't until late that afternoon, after the law had departed, that a few of Breckenridge's men rode back onto the post. They'd been working the quarter that lay in the direction of town. They'd seen the law riding by, both ways. And then, not far off the trail, they'd found where Barrett had left his horse tied up.

"Also left his guns and his uniform," reported Corporal Feeney. "We brought them back with us."

Breckenridge's eyes narrowed. "Instead of just burying them right there, is that it?" He turned away ahead of any response and ambled toward the orderly room to report. The next hostile patrol he led, Feeney was going to ride point; he'd just earned it.

"Aw, hell, Sarge," Feeney yelled after him, "I *found* them, didn't I?"

Jeff Barrett kept riding north until he realized that he really didn't know where he was. He'd been north on patrol a couple of times, but with all this land just rolling, rolling, rolling, it all looked the same.

He reined in his horse, dismounted, and started to rummage through his saddlebags. At length he came out with a packet, something wrapped in oily parchment. He unfolded the packet to reveal more folded paper. A collection of maps, actually.

Rand McNally & Company had just come out with a *Business Atlas of the Great Mississippi Valley and Pacific Slope*. On the layover in Kansas City, en route to his new assignment, recruit Barrett had spotted the maps in a store window and thought they might come in handy. He now squatted down and began to pick through them.

Hot damn. Indian Territory. But he saw that bordered on Texas, to the south, and he had a pretty fair notion he wasn't anywhere near Texas; Barrett had only a sketchy idea of geography west of the Mississippi.

Utah. Now where the hell was that? Let's see, bordered by Colorado, which meant Denver, he knew that . . . and here was the Wyoming border. Hell, that wasn't so far away.

His geography was improving.

Next he came across the California map and spent the better part of a half-hour, and much eyestrain, locating Beckwith Pass (surely there couldn't be another Beck*wourth* Pass) in the northern part.

He finally found the Wyoming map. He was beginning to think it was the only one he didn't have.

He started chewing on a piece of dried beef as he studied the map.

He found Como, where, as a recruit, he'd disembarked from the Union Pacific train. Como was some couple of hundred track miles west out of Cheyenne. His finger moved north and he found Fort Halleck. He'd heard that mentioned, but it wasn't Outpost Number Nine or regimental headquarters, he knew that much. From what he'd heard, the regimental fort was some distance northeast of Halleck, and Outpost Nine northwest, where there wasn't a damn thing on the map. Must have been too recent.

But anyway, he figured he was somewhere on the Laramie Plains, west of the Black Hills and Laramie Peak—was that Laramie Peak, way off there in the distance? —north of the railroad and east of . . . what was that, that river? The North Fork of the Platte River. Which went winding up, up, until it ran into the North Platte Wagon Road, where there was a fort nearby, Fort Casper, have to stay clear of that. . . .

Then the Platte Road, going east, bumped into the Bozeman Trail, which ran north into . . . Montana.

He dug through his maps until he found Montana.

There it was, the Bozeman, ran up into . . . damn, another fort, Fort Smith. And then . . . what was this? Reserve for the Crow Nation? Bingo! The goddamn jackpot!

Head west out of Fort Smith, up to hit the Yellowstone River, follow that winding around west and south . . . Crow agency . . . Seemed a roundabout way. Maybe he could find a shortcut.

His finger angled across the map of Wyoming, northwest, over an awful lot of mountains, to Yellowstone Park. . . .

That's funny, he thought. The West wasn't even near settled yet, much less civilized, but here somebody'd set up a park.

He could pick up the Yellowstone headwaters there, and follow the river down. . . .

Naw, that looked too damn hard. He'd go the first way.

49

Jeff Barrett stood up, folding his maps, stashing them in his saddlebags again. A wave of dizziness swept over him. He hadn't slept in three days. . . .

But he had to keep moving. The army didn't like deserters, and if they put that together with the scalped bodies in town, they'd like it even less.

But why should they connect them? Couple of renegade Indians snuck into town, that's all. But of course, a part of him wanted everybody to know that it was him, Bloody Arm, that had done the scalping. It wasn't enough that those three drunks had finally realized it.

Well, maybe he'd tell them someday. When he'd retired to his peaceful valley, revered, visited by all manner of Indian brethren, some scribe might happen by and they'd sit over black soup and share a pipe and he'd tell his story. . . .

The sun was directly overhead. (Back at Outpost Nine, Easy Company had not yet heard of the scalpings, nor found Barrett's uniform; that would come a few hours later.) Barrett mounted up and rode west.

He reached the North Fork of the Platte River by night and slept on its banks. And the next morning he recommenced his trek north, pushing his animal as hard and fast as he felt he safely could.

Windy Mandalian studied the ground in that area near the post where Barrett's horse had been tethered.

"Headed north," said Windy.

"North?" Matt Kincaid was surprised. "Thought he might head south, try to pick up a train, disappear into Utah or California."

"Headed north," repeated Windy. "Horseshoe's got a funny mark. Feller in town's got horses shod like that."

Windy tracked Barrett north, trailed by Matt and elements of First Platoon's First Squad. But after about a quarter-mile Windy reached the point where Barrett had decided to go into town and kill those men after all. Windy began to lead them toward town, depressing Matt. Maybe Barrett *had* done the scalping, wild as that might seem.

An hour later Windy was searching the ground to the rear of Gert's. He'd lost the sign just outside of town.

Now he found it again, or one just like it. "Let's have a look," he said.

They had a "look" for an hour, straight north. Hell, thought

Matt, we'll be in Montana pretty soon.

Windy stopped them where Barrett had paused to study his maps. "Spent time here, Matt, doin' *somethin'*."

"He started north," said Matt, organizing it in his mind. "Decided to head to town to get the men that had beaten him, then headed north again, got here, and . . . and what? Tried to figure out where the hell he was?"

"That's my guess, 'cause he headed west from here. Maybe he knew the Platte River was over there somewhere, had to get there to get his bearings real exact."

"Well, hell, that's good enough for me. Twenty-four-hour head start with a good horse?" Useless. "We'll head back, wire Casper to keep an eye peeled. But I'll bet he's long gone and we'll never see or hear from him again."

Barrett walked his horse slowly in among the tipis and occasional huts. The few Indians he saw, mostly women, sure weren't inspiring. They looked half-dead, about as ready to mount a war party as Dutch Rothausen and the cooks.

But then he caught a glimpse of Lame Dog and Leaf That Cries. The two war chiefs were standing off a little distance, watching him. And they were impressive. The Crow men were indeed as noble as Barrett had been led to expect.

He rode slowly toward them. These were his people. He formulated the Crow words he would speak, thankful that he'd had the foresight to study the language.

He dismounted before them. He saw that Lame Dog admired his horse. He handed Lame Dog the reins. "It is yours, my brother."

Lame Dog, initially startled to hear his tongue spoken by an apparent American, said, "I admired it. I did not want it."

"I know that," said Barrett. "Envy is not the Cr—the Sparrowhawk way. It is not your want, but my gift."

"Who are you that speak our language and know the Absaroka customs?"

"I am you . . . I wish to speak before your council."

Lame Dog saw the madness in the young man's eyes and had a feeling. But the feeling was that the times were right for madness.

"I was born of the Mountain Absaroka but stolen by the Sioux and traded to the white man. . . ."

The council was gathered, with White Moccasin at its head.

They were dubious; the Sparrowhawk looked like many things but rarely like Barrett. Nevertheless, Barrett was confident. The Crow were highly superstitious and often believed what they wanted to believe. They were thought gullible, but were probably just dreamers who sometimes failed to see where the dream ended and reality began.

"The Sioux do not steal children," said White Moccasin. "They kill them and the women. It is the Absaroka custom to spare the women and children, bring them into our tribe, and treat them as our own."

"I do not know how it happened," said Barrett, but he'd done his homework on the way north, recalling all that he'd ever read. "What you say of the Sioux is true, and I know that, for I lived with them, but it may have been that at that time their tribe was weak from losses to the Absaroka, and needed to restore their strength. What better way than to take from the powerful Absaroka?" It never hurt to tell people how great they were.

"Your words have wisdom," admitted White Moccasin. "And though you speak our language badly and do not know our signs—"

"I was too young; the white man took them from me."

"—I feel your heart is true. But why do you come to us now? What is here that is better than what you might receive as an American?"

"I come to receive nothing, but to give, to help you from this darkness, to help show you the way. My medicine is strong. I know the American. He would take everything from you, your ways, your customs, your manhood."

Lame Dog almost jumped to his feet, but Barrett continued, "I come to give them back. I start"—he reached into his bag—"with these."

He threw the three scalps down before White Moccasin, who immediately recognized them as having belonged to Americans, and his heart skipped. "But these are of Americans."

"Yes," hissed Barrett, "but the days when the Absaroka must only count coups among the hated Sioux and Blackfoot are gone. An enemy to equal them is the American. We fought for years by their side, did we not? And our reward for that is to have our ancient lands seized, our tobacco planting lands taken, our horses stolen, our heritage denied. Locked into this poor stretch of land, our warriors are expected to live like women. I know the American, his ways, the way he fights. I can help the great chief of the Absaroka, White Moccasin, lead his people to victory and a new land."

Truly, if a donkey had appeared among them with similar claims and promises, the Sparrowhawk might have felt tempted to adopt it as one of their own.

"His words are true and brave, White Moccasin," said Lame Dog. "Though he may not be full-blooded Absaroka, his words bespeak a goodly portion of true blood. He has proven himself a warrior. Let him prove his wisdom, his medicine."

"His medicine is not as great as mine," argued White Moccasin.

"But his medicine is that of the *warrior*," argued Lame Dog. "It is not that of counsel, of tobacco-planting. And this very day," he lied, "I feel that the seeds you planted have begun to grow."

"How can we identify you?" asked White Moccasin of Barrett. "If you were once Sparrowhawk, and the Great Spirit has sent you to this tribe, you may still have family. Have you no special signs that may mark you as a woman's child?"

Barrett knew he was home free, but he did not think in that manner; instead he giddily sensed the guidance of a hand and spirit greater than any in the tribal council. White Moccasin was right, the Great Spirit *was* present.

Also present, on Barrett, were a vast multitude of moles of varying size. Surely some would match those of a lost child. He mentioned the moles.

He was then poked and prodded by just about every older woman in the entire village. At length, two small moles behind his right ear, both on the rear portion of the lobe, offered proof positive that he belonged to the family of Fire Fox, the particular woman being an elderly crone named Pretty Feet, a woman who'd been through many wars and who had only four complete fingers remaining. One of those missing joints presumably fell many years earlier when her baby boy, Fawn Eyes, disappeared in a Sioux raid.

Gifts, meager but heartfelt, were showered upon Fire Fox, Pretty Feet, and the prodigal son, Barrett/Fawn Eyes.

"Your words have swelled our hearts," said Lame Dog later. "But the way will be difficult. We are surrounded by enemies. The American fort, Keogh, with its fierce commander, Miles,

53

is not far away to the north and east."

"Hear me," said Barrett. "Colonel Miles will not pursue our people, now so small in numbers. He has his eyes on greater things. General Howard is presently engaging our friends, the Nez Perce. Colonel Miles awaits the summons to join that battle. He will not see us leave, or if he does, he will make himself blind."

"Your words are good, Fawn Eyes," said Lame Dog.

"But we must prepare well," cautioned Barrett. He wasn't all that happy with the name Fawn Eyes—it hardly had a martial sound—but he expected to change it soon. "We must be careful."

And so, with words of patience and caution, but also of vengeance, Jeff Barrett began his life with the Crow.

eight ─────────────

"Goddammit, I been robbed *again!*"

Weasel nearly jumped a mile.

Landing back down on his bunk, he looked around. Down the barracks a ways, Private Musselman, normally reddish-hued, had practically turned scarlet. "I had a necklace here what b'longed to my mama." His eyes searched for and found Private Gillies. Weasel stared right back. His own mother had been a whore, decidedly lacking a heart of gold, so he couldn't fully appreciate the excitement. But when the whole other end of the barracks started heading his way, led by Musselman and Parker, he vamoosed to the doorway, where he stood and watched.

The men tore his bunk and belongings apart, determined to find proof.

When they didn't, Gillies raged from the doorway, "You better put all that stuff back t'gether again."

"In a pig's eye!"

"I think you better do it," insinuated the calm, deceptively soft voice of Sergeant Chubb, "or you'll be diggin' a trench from here to regimental HQ."

Chubb, unmarried, had a small room at one end of the barracks (First Platoon's Sergeant Olsen had one too, at the other end). The last couple of days, Chubb had kept a low profile and half an eye on Private Gillies, and was pretty sure that if the necklace had been stolen, Weasel hadn't been the culprit. "You sure you didn't just mislay it? You'd mislay your head, Mussel, if it warn't attached."

"Didn't mislay it. Allus keep it in a box."

Chubb sat down on the edge of a bunk and didn't speak for a while. But finally he observed mildly, "I don't see no one straightenin' out Private Gillies' belongings."

Matt Kincaid was on edge. Inactivity did it to him. He sat behind his desk, carving slivers from the desktop.

"Let me know when you need a new desk," came Sergeant Cohen's voice from the orderly room.

"What kind of wood's this?" Matt called out.

"Birch, most likely. Hard goin', huh? I'll order you a pine one next. That's softer."

Matt grunted. Then he heard noise from the parade. He went outside, grimacing at Ben Cohen on the way.

A wagon train of supplies had just pulled in, about twenty-five to thirty wagons, in units of three and four. That is, three or four wagons were hooked together to form a unit that was drawn by anywhere from nine to twelve yoke of bull oxen.

The army—for this train came from HQ—was kind of cheap that way. Or sensible. Horse or mule trains were faster than bull trains, but the animals had to be grain-fed. And horses and mules were also fair game for Mr. Lo when he was looking to enlarge or replenish his stock. Bulls were slower but could be grazed, thereby saving a lot of feed weight. And Mr. Lo wasn't interested in oxen. What he could get from them, he could get easier and better from buffalo. So any train paid for by the army was almost sure to be drawn by oxen.

Each three- or four-wagon unit could carry from seven to ten tons of freight. In each unit, a long, heavy chain extended from the first two oxen down the center of the team to the lead wagon. Every pair of animals, with the exception of the pair nearest the wagon, was attached to this chain.

The lead pair of animals were usually the smallest of the lot and chosen for their intelligence. The ones behind them were called the swing team. And the last pair, attached directly to the tongue of the first wagon, which they both pulled and guided, were called wheelers. They were usually the biggest and the strongest of all.

A horse or mule train might make twenty miles a day. A bull train made less.

With a bull train, the bullwhackers rolled out at daybreak, hooked up the oxen, and started rolling. They'd stop at about

9:00 A.M., turn the oxen loose to graze, and prepare breakfast and take care of odd jobs. Around noon they'd start the train up again and drive until about four, when they'd stop and turn the oxen loose again to graze. After a while they'd hook up again and drive until it got too dark to see. For this, with no time off for Sundays or holidays, the bullwhacker got about fifty dollars a month—a hell of a lot more than the U.S. Army recruits' thirteen dollars a month, but the job was a hell of a lot harder.

Seeing the arrival of the train, Matt thought he might duck into the sutler's, maybe chew some fat with the bullwhackers.

He saw Clara Plowright seated outside of the sutler's. Her legs were kind of spread and the print dress she wore sagged between them. Matt reflected that married women sometimes forgot about being chaste and ladylike; they figured they were already married and no one else would be interested. Like as not they figured wrong. Of course, in Clara Plowright's case, it might not be just carelessness. And when Clara tried to catch his eye he became a bit more certain.

Inside the sutler's, he encountered Maggie Cohen, who asked in a low voice, "You see Clara out there?"

Matt nodded and Maggie shook her head slowly and murmured, "I'm not sure Sergeant Plowright knows how to handle a woman like that."

Even though Matt agreed he was surprised, and he was made a trifle uncomfortable by hearing it from Maggie Cohen. Maggie was continually surprising him.

The bullwhackers were doing some asking around about hostiles. They'd heard that Mr. Lo had started kicking his heels up some, even slipped into town nearby and got himself some coups. "Glad we're usin' bulls. Hate to have to pull these wagons my own damn self." The speaker laughed. "Missin' a scalp b'sides."

Matt shook his head. "No activity as far as I know. And that business in town's kind of a puzzle."

"How so?"

"Can't figure out who the hell the hostiles are or where they came from. Or why they did it."

"Ain'tcha got no hostiles around here?"

"We've got a lot of friendlies."

"Friendly, huh?" roared one bullwhacker, and he laughed as he made a slashing motion at his own throat.

Matt went back outside. Sergeant Cohen, Skinflint Wilson—the supply sergeant who doubled as ordnance—and the sutler, Pop Evans, were moving among the wagon train, checking off items on sheets of paper and directing their dispersal by a group of enlistees, plus two of the sutler's help.

"Sergeant Cohen," called Matt, "when you get a chance, have Private Enright report to me."

Private Jeremy Enright stood uneasily before Matt Kincaid's desk. As far as he knew, he hadn't done anything wrong; in fact, he'd done everyone a favor by turning up the cross-burners, Popper and Kazmaier.

"Tell me what you know about Barrett."

"Good soldier, sir. Hard worker, did his share. Handled a gun well. Never spoke poorly of others, 'ceptin'—"

"Enright, the man's not up for a commission. He's a deserter. He might have killed and scalped three men in town. And I don't understand one bit of it. I'd like to try to get a line on him. Now, I was watching you the night the cross was burned. You didn't know who did it . . . *then* . . . but I'm sure you knew who it was meant for. How'd you know?"

Enright, with some reluctance, described his conversation with Barrett outside the privy, and described the fight that had led to it, and what had led to the fight.

Matt said, "You mean, at first Barrett sounded like a bona fide Klansman himself?"

"Sure did. If he hadn't told me what he did tell me later on, I would've voted him the most likely to have set the fire."

"Why'd he tell you?"

"Who else was he going to tell? Not that I welcomed it, but this ain't the most tolerant bunch I've ever seen. Got a lot of these 'galvanized Yankees,' I think that's what they're called."

"Johnny Rebs? Ex-Confederates? Yeah, that's exactly what they're called," Matt affirmed.

"Runs afoul of the canned beef sometimes."

"Canned beef?" Matt smiled. "Yeah, galvanized pigs, I can see how it might."

"But I figure it was just gettin' to him, sir," said Enright. "A lot of pressure. And I'm older, steadier I guess, and I'm a private like him. That's probably why he picked me to unload on."

Matt thought that sounded right. "But what were these dates he gave out?"

"I remember pretty clear. I was listening close. It was strange, strange enough to remember. Born the 26th of April in Fredericksburg—"

"What year?"

"Didn't say."

"According to his records here," Matt said, shuffling some papers, "He was born in September. The fourteenth. 1854."

"That figures, sir, because the *second* time he was born, in 1866, he said he was twelve."

Matt scratched his head, and kept on scratching until his hair was rumpled. "And one of thirteen children too, that was the number, wasn't it?"

"Yessir. Thirteen."

"Doesn't make sense. Records don't say anything about any brothers or sisters. In fact, no kin at all . . . put his birthplace as St. Louis. . . . Was he crazy?"

"No more'n anybody else here, sir. Not enough to scare you, anyway. At least he didn't scare *me,* sir."

Very little scared Enright, thought Matt.

"Which ain't to say, sir, that he didn't get a little spooky sometimes," Enright went on. "Like the last night I saw him, he sat outside in the parade all night. Said he was medi . . . medi . . . he was waiting for a dream or vision or something."

"A vision? What the hell did Barrett think he was, wondered Matt, a Negro or Indian?

"Did he get one?" Matt asked.

"If he did, sir, he didn't tell me."

"Fine, Enright. Thanks. You can go."

John "Weasel" Gillies nearly jumped a mile again. Second time that day.

There he'd been, in the rear of the stables, catching a little shut-eye atop the sacks of grain, when something touched him. He hadn't come out of the New York slums without a healthy fear and respect for rats. And someone had told him these Western rats were near as poisonous as rattlers.

He was down off the pile of sacks and rolling on the ground before he looked up and saw little Billy looking down at him.

"You sure are jumpy," said Billy.

"Why the hell you push me off like that? An' what the hell

59

you doin' followin' me aroun'?" But the bluster had no punch to it. Gillies couldn't really bring himself to dislike a boy who, nearly full grown, was still smaller than him, and who acted nearly as untrustworthy as Gillies looked. "Aw, shit, come on down here, kid. I don't feel like yellin'."

Billy slid down.

"Been keepin' an eye out," said Billy.

"Oh, yeah? What fer?"

"Feller what's been stealin' that stuff."

Gillies looked at him with greater interest. "So?"

Billy stared at him earnestly. "I'll get him, don't you worry. Ain't no one that can sneak aroun' like me."

"Well, fer Chrissakes, don't let 'em *catch* you sneakin' aroun'. Where you from, Billy? You got folks?"

nine _____

Fawn Eyes/Jeff Barrett sat on the banks of the Big Boulder River. He'd been there all day, clad only in a breech-clout, walking about at times, sitting crosslegged at others. He had told the other Absaroka that his warrior medicine was upon him and that he needed to meditate in order to receive his vision. They'd respected his need and left him alone by the running water.

The water wasn't running swiftly enough, though. The place was a plague of mosquitoes and flies. He wished he'd sought some lofty height for his meditation.

The truth was, he was bored. And in that lay the danger. Kept busy, mind and body, he was a pretty stable fellow. But when he was idle, his latent madness—complicated, perhaps, by the concussion he'd received in the fight with the teamsters—seized the moment and his fantasies soared. They'd been soaring more of late. In fact, they'd begun to soar even when he was busy.

And such insistent possession, instead of worrying him, led him to accept the self-evident truth of his visions; the strength of such seizures could only be that of Truth.

Then too, when he accepted, when he felt under the spell of his visions, there was an undeniable sense of release. And that also had to mean they were good and right. Such was his understandable, if flawed, logic.

He looked to the heavens. Night was falling. He saw a star just above the horizon, the first star. Atmospheric conditions produced an aureole around the star and he took this as a sign.

He retraced his steps to the Crow village.

It was full night before he spoke before the council.

"Hear me. I have seen the white man's path and it leads to the banks of a deep body of water. And from that water springs a wall of fire. And the earth has fallen away behind us. And strange, wild creatures did occupy that small piece of remaining land and did drive the Sparrowhawk people into the flaming lake...."

As he spoke he began to see it himself. And it was convincing.

"We must leave the white man's path. Tonight. There is a land of ease and buffalo and hunting and battles with our enemies...."

They took him seriously. The Crow, like many Indian tribes, always had trouble arguing with dreams. To them, a dream seemed to represent a reality beyond dispute.

"Where would we go?" wondered White Moccasin.

"Where the Great Spirit leads us."

White Moccasin frowned. The Great Spirit hadn't been showing *him* any particular path. But perhaps it was because he had not looked hard enough. He saw the eagerness upon the faces of his council and he raised his arms and bowed his head, willing a vision to come forth.

He saw the tobacco-planting ceremony, which was his claim to power and influence.

"Yes," he said, lowering his arms, his face becoming serene, "Fawn Eyes speaks truly, and I have seen the way."

Jeff Barrett/Fawn Eyes felt a swell of excitement. It was easier than he'd thought it would be.

"We have no horses, few guns," said Lame Dog. "What does your medicine say to that?"

White Moccasin thought that properly fell under the category of warrior medicine, and he looked to Fawn Eyes.

"There are plenty of horses at the agency," said Barrett. "We already have a few guns, our lances, and our arrows. We will be shown the way to more guns." Just get 'em moving, he thought, that's all, just get 'em moving.

Fifteen minutes later Fawn Eyes—damn that name!—Lame Dog, Buffalo Hump, and three younger men left for the agency. The Crow rode well and easily—they were superb horsemen—while Fawn Eyes faked it as best he could. Actually, by the

62

time they reached the agency, Barrett had improved.

It was still before midnight, but the agency was dark. The horses, more than a hundred of them, milled quietly in a huge corral situated some distance behind and to the side of the agency. The agent was not such a horse lover as to want the beasts standing nearby, watching him eat, nor did he care for the fumes from their droppings, nor for the flies that the droppings lured in swarms.

The horses had been seized from various Indian tribes, including the Crow. About half were the smaller Indian pony, a hardy, grazing animal, and the rest were reclaimed army horses, animals that fared poorly as grazers but were larger and stronger when properly grained. Barrett decided he'd see they were properly fed. They took them all.

The Crow horsemen easily found a few leaders, bound their noses with cloth, and walked them quietly out of the corral. The rest followed docilely.

Barrett figured that the agent, or friends of the agent, had intended to make a tidy profit selling the horses. He smiled. He imagined the reaction when they found their profits gone, stolen. Or, as the Crow would claim, either reclaimed or, at worst, merely *borrowed*. Fragile distinctions, thought Barrett, but then he had to kick his mount into a run as the horses, well clear now, were beginning to move faster.

Lame Dog and his confederates herded the horses expertly back to the Crow encampment with nary a loss. The Sparrowhawk wanted to celebrate their sudden enrichment, but Fawn Eyes and White Moccasin cut them off, insisting on immediate departure.

There was time, though, for Fawn Eyes' proud father to give him another name, that of Big Horse. It wasn't much better than Fawn Eyes, thought Barrett, but it was a move in the right direction.

Barrett had read, in the Culbertson manuscript back in St. Louis, that a Crow village was able to fold its tents, fashion travois, load everything up, and be on the move in twenty minutes or less.

Less, guessed Barrett. He wished he'd bought himself a watch. But then, near naked as he was, where would he hang the damned thing?

Lame Dog rode up. "Big Horse will show us the way."

Who the hell was Big Horse? wondered Barrett for a moment. Then he remembered; he was going to have to start writing these names down before it got out of hand. "White Moccasin knows the way," he said, passing the buck.

And White Moccasin, having talked himself fully into *his* vision, did indeed know.

He led them through the night, directly west. They soon encountered the Yellowstone River, then turned and rode upriver, climbing slowly into the mountains.

They came to Yellowstone City, a mountain town with all of twenty-five known inhabitants (the maps Barrett possessed included the latest census estimates). Barrett didn't think that their nearly two hundred Crow had much to fear from a city teeming with twenty-five whites, but he and White Moccasin thought it foolish to announce their presence and direction by riding right through the settlement. The Americans tended to be very excitable. So they rode around.

The Crow village was traveling fast. Usually, again according to those old manuscripts, a traveling village covered anywhere from ten to twenty miles a day. But that was only if they weren't hurrying. Barrett thought that *this* village was doing a hell of a lot better than that. They'd made Yellowstone City by dawn, which was moving smartly. Their only priority was speed, not comfort. The agency would know by now that their horses were missing. It would take them a while for their Indian trackers (if there were any Indian trackers, since they usually came to White Moccasin for such men) to trace the horses to the Crow village. And it wouldn't be until then that they discovered that White Moccasin and his tribe had vanished. Then they'd have to figure out where they'd gone.

It would take time—more time than if they were the highly suspect, warlike Sioux, who were expected to jump reservations, rather than the "peaceable" Crow—and that time had to be put to good use.

But White Moccasin had been wise. The Americans would not expect them to choose the most difficult path of escape, through the towering mountains. That would cause the Americans even further delay, as they sought to credit their senses, or their scouts' senses. But they still had to move fast.

Some short distance upriver from Yellowstone City, Emigrant Creek joined the Yellowstone River and Barrett saw that his map, so far, was accurate. That meant that two towns lay ahead of them, Emigrant on the far side of the river and Emigrant Gulch on their side. And that would be the last they'd see of settlements for a long while.

Barrett made a quick estimate of guns and ammo. They didn't have much, or not enough, anyway.

"We need guns and ammunition," he advised White Moccasin. "There is a small settlement ahead."

"But they are Americans," objected White Moccasin, still in thrall to his erstwhile comrades, the white man.

Barrett felt his temperature rise. The white man. He, a black man who had tried to be white, now despised the name, the words, the race. "They are no longer your friends," he argued forcefully. "You know what happened at the Red Cloud agency, at the Spotted Tail. The Absaroka were cast aside when the company was formed under Lieutenant South and the ranks were filled with Cheyenne." Barrett had heard some men of Easy Company discussing the matter, the reliable Matt Kincaid in particular. "*Not* the Sparrowhawk, who had proven their friendship and valor, but the Cheyenne, who had fought the American to the death. The Americans are your friends no more." He added bitterly, "They never were."

But White Moccasin, a man of peace and patience, held fast. There would be no killing of Americans. But they *would* get their guns.

White Moccasin proceeded to demonstrate his mastery of the American mentality, especially when it came to small, isolated settlements on the frontier. An hour later the twenty-five-odd inhabitants of the settlement looked up from their activities to find some fifty to seventy-five mounted warriors, all armed with guns or bows, placidly watching them. A massacre seemed imminent.

White Moccasin rode out in front. "We are going to the mountains," he said, "to live in peace. But we must hunt to live. We need guns and ammunition. We will give you fine horses in exchange, and some of our younger people to live among you and work with you and learn American ways. Our power will also protect you from attack by unfriendly tribes."

The town of Emigrant Gulch couldn't do enough for them. They were swamped with guns and ammunition. The townspeople refused the offer of Absaroka youngsters, as White Moccasin had known they would, but selected a number of fine horses.

The Crow rode away smiling.

And it worked out rather well for the town. Eight days later they were attacked by an unfriendly tribe—possibly renegade Flathead—and though they were not rescued by White Moccasin, as promised, and though the guns and ammo he'd taken made defense difficult, the swift horses he'd exchanged did make flight feasible and successful. Afterwards, in safety, the former inhabitants of Emigrant Gulch didn't know whether to curse or praise White Moccasin.

Big Horse, along with the other members of the council, praised White Moccasin to the mountaintops where they were headed and to the skies above and beyond. Big Horse, in fact, was rather amazed. He'd thought White Moccasin one of those miserable, mealymouthed "good" Indians. But now he concluded that while the old man might still lack a taste for war and killing, and might be one part mealymouthed, he was most assuredly nine parts guile, knowledgeable and clever. If he ever took to actual fighting, put his mind to strategy and tactics, he might be a force to reckon with. But that was a big *if*, one that Barrett did not plan to count on.

Entering the Yellowstone Park, at the foot of Sepulchre Mountain where Black Tail Deer Creek ran into the now diminutive Yellowstone, they finally paused to rest and hunt.

After hunting and eating their fill, they slept the night and the next morning got under way again.

They retraced the course of the ever-shrinking river until they came to the enormous alpine Yellowstone Lake.

This entire stretch was one of wonder. They had often heard tales of Yellowstone's thunderous, pluming geysers, its varicolored paint pots, and its foaming mud springs, but only a few warriors in this present group had ever witnessed the various spectacles. Never had a full village found its way there.

The Crow were like children as they frolicked their way around the western shore of the lake, partaking of the mud baths and waiting with bated breath for the geysers.

Could this be the wondrous land meant for them by the Great Spirit?

Big Horse, growing bored again and waxing mystical, said no. And White Moccasin, though tempted, also said no; he sensed that the promised land would be a new land, beyond the old lands of the Crow Nation. It would be a land where buffalo and true enemies, such as the Blackfoot (for he knew they were moving away from the Sioux), would abound. To say nothing of its being a land where the winter's snow did not measure many times the height of a man.

But beyond all that, White Moccasin also had his special vision in mind. That had to be tended to first.

They continued south.

ten

"Hey, Dobbsy me boy, tell me again how that horse doctor fixed you up. An' be sure to be leavin' the screams an' cryin' in." Private Malone wasn't drunk, so his Irish lilt was still intelligible.

Private Stretch Dobbs wasn't drunk either, so he merely made a long, lugubrious face and pointed it at Malone.

"Hell, Stretch, that was *after*. Gimme the full treatment."

It was the noon grub break at Outpost Number Nine, and Easy Company's two most dependable cutups, Privates Malone and Dobbs, had eaten just enough of Dutch Rothausen's leftovers to stay alive and had hustled to the barracks to rest up; grading roads was no picnic.

"We just got a whole damn wagon train of food. When the hell do you think Dutch'll get around to dishing it out?"

"Soon's it gets old and moldy enough," was Stretch's sour response. His pecker was still not fully recovered, so he still approached peeing with trepidation.

"Hey! Who the hell's that down there?" cried Malone.

"Where?"

"Down *there*, hidin' in with all them buffalo coats, dummy." Heavy-haired buffalo-skin coats weren't standard gear for the Wyoming winter, the way they were up in Montana—Colonel Miles' men, on winter patrol, looked like a herd of buffalo, and Mr. Lo often treated them as such—but a number of Easy's men, on their own, had treated themselves to some. "Bet we found us our thief. Lemme see what a few bullets into them hides will get me."

68

Little Billy came leaping out, alarmed and mad as a hornet at the same time. "I ain't no thief, dammit."

"Look like one t' me," said Malone.

"'Cept," said Dobbs, "tiny as he is, he kin only steal somethin' little—"

"Like your pecker?"

"Like your asshole!"

"You been *peekin'!*" Malone appeared outraged at Stretch's reference to his chronic constipation.

Billy slipped back out of sight.

"Hey. Who said you could disappear again?"

Billy popped back out, pissed off at these two nuisances. "If you'd jes' shut up and lemme alone, I might jes' catch me a thief."

"And get Weasel off the hook, huh? Go ahead, I don't think Weasel's done it neither. Hell, I grown up with punks like that an' they don't steal no cheap necklaces. Jeez! Steal yer shoes, yer money, somethin' valuable, not that cheap piece o' shit Musselman had hid," Dobbs said.

Billy retired and Malone and Dobbs lay back.

Sure was warm and drowsy-like this fine afternoon.

"You boys seen Sergeant Plowright?"

Their eyes snapped open.

Clara Plowright was standing there, looking down at them. She was wearing a cotton dress and it looked like she had nothing on underneath. Malone struggled to sit up, mopping his brow. Dobbs felt a dull ache in his groin. "Sure is hot, isn't it?" she remarked.

"Sure is," croaked Malone. "Sergeant Plowright? I think I last saw him with *you*."

"Ol' Blowhard?" said Dobbs to Malone. "He was out there stringin' wire. He was the one had Weasel do all them pushups."

There was a muffled sound from among the buffalo coats.

"Blowhard?" repeated Clara, amused.

Dobbs stared at her. "Did I say that?" He guessed he had. "That's 'cause he works so hard, always breathin' up a storm. You know, *blowing hard?*" And Dobbs huffed and puffed a demonstration.

"I figure he'll be along any second now," said Malone, trying to rescue the situation. "Whyn't you set a spell?" He got up as if to offer her his bed.

"Well," she said, smiling, "don't mind if—"

At that moment, infuriatingly, Reb McBride blew a call to assembly.

If Reb was having fun, thought Malone furiously, he'd kill the cracker bastard.

The two men reluctantly left the barracks.

Back a while, about the time that Dobbs and Malone were ducking into the barracks, a message came over the telegraph. Four Eyes Bradshaw, the bespectacled company clerk, took the message.

Once he'd written it down, he stared at it for a while, then tapped out a request for a repeat.

He got it, and it left him shaking his head. There wasn't anyone else in the orderly room, but although the message seemed strange, it didn't seem particularly urgent, so he just waited until someone showed up.

Ben Cohen came back first. He read the message. "Try to get a confirmation on this," he told Bradshaw.

"I already did, Sarge," he said proudly.

Cohen nodded his head, mumbling, "Good for you, good for you."

Lieutenants Allison and Price wandered in next, for want of anywhere better to go, followed moments later by Lieutenant Smaldoon. Cohen didn't show any of them the message; he was saving it for Captain Conway. He did suggest, though, that the officers hang around, making it sound ominous. Mr. Price suddenly thought of lots of places where it would be better to be just then.

Matt Kincaid showed up next and, sunk in gloom, went into his office and resumed carving up the desk.

Ben Cohen wondered if Captain Conway hadn't called it a day and nipped back to his quarters and Flora for a leisurely afternoon in bed.

But then Captain Conway strode in with that rolling, foot-soldier's gait that a lifetime of sporadic riding had failed to conquer. Immediately he noticed the assembled officers and the serious faces.

Cohen handed him the message. "Reservation jump, sir."

Conway scanned the message and murmured disbelievingly, "Crow?"

"What?" squawked Matt, coming out of his office.

70

"Is this right, Sergeant?"

"Checked it, sir. It's Crow, all right. Says 'White Moccasin' right there, sir."

"But I met White Moccasin once," Conway said. "He seemed to me about as hostile as my Aunt Sally. And the Crow . . . they wouldn't do a thing like that, they've always been friends of the white man."

"Either they were friends," said Matt, "or they figured that was better than getting killed by the white man. Or maybe it was just a matter of them getting off on the right foot with the white man and it became a tradition. The Crow are superstitious, and I remember reading that when the white man first showed up, the Crow thought he had a lot of magic. Big medicine. Guns and all that. And then it worked out pretty well for the Crow; when supplies came down they usually got first crack. And when it came to guns, they got better ones than the Sioux or Blackfoot; helped them kill 'em better."

"Think that's all there was to it?" wondered Warner Conway, feeling somehow let down. He glanced at the message again. "I can tell you from this that the War Department's about fit to be tied. The Sioux they expect to do something wrong, and the same goes for the Cheyenne and damn near all the rest. But the Crow . . . they figure they've been backstabbed by their favorite cousin, the one they've done so much for."

"Yeah, like Matt said, haven't killed them," drawled Windy Mandalian, who'd slipped in unnoticed.

"Aw c'mon, Windy, Matt's not the only one who knows how unfair it's been," objected Warner Conway.

"Fight alongside us, scout for us, any old damn thing," droned Matt, "and end up crammed onto a reservation the same as every other red bastard who couldn't kill enough of us."

"And get their horses taken besides," said Windy. "And that *hurts*. Hell, to them, horses is the next best thing to buffalo, maybe even better. They don't think they're nothin' without horses."

"Well, they got horses back," said Conway, eyeing the message.

"Well goddamn good for them," said Windy.

"Don't go celebrating too quick," said Conway. "We're going to have to go get them."

Allison and Price, picking up the prevailing mood, groaned. But Smaldoon smiled tightly.

71

"How come?" wondered Matt Kincaid. "They must have jumped off in Montana, that's where the reservation is. What's wrong with Fort Ellis—that's right nearby—or Keogh? Seems to me that Miles would love to run down some helpless Crow."

Conway stiffened. "Goddammit, Matt, I didn't hear that. And neither did anyone else," he added as a warning.

"Now," he resumed, after breathing deeply, "as it happens, there *are* patrols out from Ellis and Keogh. But it turns out that instead of heading in any expected direction, the Crow headed south. Into Yellowstone. Probably all the way down through it. And that makes them ours."

"Great," said Matt, "that's just great. There are some real hostiles out there somewhere, and we've got to go nursemaid some unhappy Crow back to a lousy reservation."

"Orders, Matt, orders."

"Well, sir," said Matt, "I figure Mr. Allison or one of them can handle it. I'm going to carve up some more desk."

"Hold on, Matt. I want you to go."

Kincaid turned slowly in his office doorway and stared at Captain Conway. Conway eyed him levelly. "You, Matt. I'm not completely happy with the sound of this."

Matt continued to eye him. But Matt also knew that Captain Conway, despite his purebred Anglo-Saxon look and manner, had a feel for the Indian that many a half-breed lacked. Matt was curious. "You figure there's a joker in there somewhere?"

Captain Conway nodded, but then his mood abruptly shifted, as if to dispel the funereal atmosphere. "Any of you men want some whiskey?" he asked, addressing everybody with the possible exception of Corporal Bradshaw, whose losing bouts with beer were near legend.

"Some of your own, sir?" Matt asked, and Conway nodded. "From the family vineyard?"

"Flora's family vineyard. They keep us supplied. Finest bourbon I've ever tasted."

There was pouring and some drinking.

"Ay-men," said Matt, "nothing finer. Glad we didn't lose the South. Might've missed some good sipping."

"Now," said Captain Conway, "about that joker . . . As I said, I've met White Moccasin, but I've also met several of his seconds-in-command, so to speak. Lame Dog and Spotted Elk scouted for me. And I'm certain that none of them would have gone off on their own. Some kind of renegade, red or white, led them off. And that's the unpredictable factor, Matt, and that's why I want you out there. We need your experience, just in case."

"You're sure about that, sir?" asked Matt. "That renegade stuff?"

"No, Matt, of course I'm not sure, but I *think* so, and you're going."

Matt sighed and said, "Have you got any other ideas?"

"Yes, and this doesn't depend on the renegade, but rather on the route they've taken. The Crow are tobacco-planters. They get their medicine from that, or rather, the tobacco-planters are their medicine men."

"Yes, I've heard that," said Matt, "and Montana's lousy for tobacco. At least I've never heard of any growing there."

"Well, it's not very good tobacco, as we know tobacco. It chews terrible, but it smokes tolerable."

"So where'd they plant it, usually?"

"At the base of the Wind River Mountains, where the Wind River runs into the Big Horn."

"Meaning that if they slid down out of the Yellowstone, they could pick up the Wind at its head and follow it down."

"Be pretty easy," said Windy.

"Sure would. Well, Captain"—Matt grinned—"it's been a while since I've been up that way."

"Oh, and Matt," Conway said, taking Matt aside after the orderly room had emptied, "something's been bothering me. Maybe you have a suggestion. This Plowright woman, Clara—seems to me that she's headed for trouble."

Jesus, thought Matt, the captain did have a sharp eye. Or . . .

"She hasn't . . . ?" Matt broke off tactfully.

"To *me?*" Conway grinned. "No, I have just seen things."

"Well, sir, you're right . . . but I don't have the answer."

Conway nodded slowly. "Pity," he said.

Later that afternoon, Matt Kincaid rode out of Outpost Number Nine at the head of a platoon of men. Actually, they weren't all from one platoon, but it was a platoon-sized detachment.

He took the First Squad from his usual First Platoon, which included Malone and Dobbs—Dobbs's sore pecker notwithstanding—plus privates Holzer, Rottweiler, fair-haired Weatherby, Parker, Medwick, Felson, Carter, and the squad leader, Corporal Miller. But for platoon sergeant he took Sergeant

Chubb, in part because Chubb was a good man to have along, but also because he wanted to take men from Chubb's Third Platoon, namely Sergeant Plowright.

He'd chosen Plowright, thinking that his absence might help bring his relationship with his wife to some kind of head. That dumb woman, hot and frustrated, might do something really foolish, show her true colors, and open Blowhard's eyes. Of course, Matt also had a strong hunch that Blowhard's eyes were sealed shut pretty permanently.

But Kazmaier and Popper were in Blowhard's squad. With any luck they might get their asses blown off.

Some fifteen other men, from Blowhard's squad and Third Platoon's Second Squad, rounded out the troop.

Matt considered dragging one of the second lieutenants along, but he didn't like Smaldoon, and Price was of minimal value, and Allison was too valuable.

Windy went along too. He also was too valuable, but too valuable to be left behind.

"Crow, huh?" muttered Windy, and spat desultorily. "How excitin'."

Matt, riding beside him, hoped there might be a surprise in store. But if he'd known exactly how many surprises they would in fact encounter, he might not have been so light-hearted.

eleven

A few days before Matt's departure with his men, White Moccasin, Big Horse, and the Crow had moved down out of Yellowstone, traveling southeast until they picked up a tributary of the Wind.

They'd followed that stream, making good time, until they met the Wind, down which they then rode. The land grew increasingly familiar to White Moccasin and any of his people who were old enough to have been there for the last tobacco-planting ceremony.

But, though moving swiftly, they also moved carefully. Both Little Deer and Waterfly, celebrated war chiefs, rode well in front, doing the scouting that normally might be left to men of lesser stature. It had been many a season since the Crow had been on any warpath, and riding free ahead of the main body, scouting, gave both men a sense of exhilaration and purpose. Their horses trod with surefooted ease through the shrubbery and low trees on the banks of the river, as they kept their eyes peeled for sign.

And it was fortunate that they were so alert, because they almost ran into a band of Cheyenne. They pulled up in time, though, crept forward, satisfied themselves that it was indeed a small Cheyenne war party, and then turned back and rode silently for the main body of Crow.

"How many?" asked Big Horse/Barrett. White Moccasin had retired to the background. He would speak only if questioned or if he thought an egregious error was about to be committed.

75

"Small," said Little Deer. "Twelve."

"Guns?"

"Many more than they number."

"Which means they are good, since they have already killed men with guns." Big Horse let that warning sink in; he had no idea how impetuous these men might be. "We must be careful."

"The Sparrowhawk are always careful."

Barrett assumed command and chose thirty men to go with him, including all the war chiefs. He made sure that each man had a rifle, a lance or hatchet, and a knife. He himself tucked one of his two Scoffs into his waistband—he was the only man of all the Crow to have pistols, and he was glad he'd hung onto them. Of course, he too carried a rifle, a hatchet, and a knife besides. He felt pretty damn dangerous.

An hour later they had crept through the shrubs and tall grass almost to within scent of the Cheyenne. The Cheyenne weren't, Barrett realized, immemorial enemies of the Crow, but they were friendly with the hated Sioux, and would do. It was time for the Crow to be blooded, and any blood, really, would serve the purpose. And having heard no objections to killing these Cheyenne, he assumed that sentiment was unanimous.

Barrett's instinct was to decimate the Cheyenne from cover, but the Indian way, he knew, was to close with the enemy and take them in hand-to-hand combat. It was for that reason that to return with many coups without having lost any of one's own men was so honorable. Mr. Lo might be foolish, but he was brave.

So it was that at a signal from Barrett/Big Horse, the thirty Crow leaped from cover and, with bloodcurdling howls, fell upon the unsuspecting Cheyenne.

Slyly, Barrett actually gave the signal when he was already moving. Consequently, he got to a half-risen Cheyenne first and, obvious to all, was the first to cut the enemy. It was a bit more than a cut, actually; he buried his hatchet in the back of the Cheyenne's skull.

He then set about scalping the dead man, hoping his lack of dexterity was not also noted. If he didn't get any better at it, he thought, he'd have to follow the lead of Crazy Horse and declare himself uninterested in the taking of scalps.

Once the coups were counted, a messenger was sent back

to summon the rest of the Crow.

They arrived, led by White Moccasin, in less than an hour. Upon viewing the grisly remnants of the slaughter, they all commenced to dance and celebrate.

And Lame Dog proclaimed that Big Horse had been the first to cut the enemy, proclaiming it happily since envy was a characteristic foreign to the Crow.

Barrett watched, somewhat sadly, as his "father," Fire Fox, gladly gave away all his belongings. Barrett felt better, though, when members of the tribe later showered Fire Fox with gifts and thus replenished his holdings.

It was certainly a peculiar rite, thought Barrett, but obviously a sacred one. And he recalled reading how the mulatto Beckwith had almost ruined his poor father with his success in battle. Barrett smiled, and then it occurred to him that this was a good time for another name.

Not leaving anything to chance, he took his "father" aside and suggested as much, even going so far as to suggest the name Bloody Arm. His "father" agreed, and so it was done.

The dancing went on and on. It was beginning to get tiresome when Barrett, or Bloody Arm, went to White Moccasin and said they shouldn't stay there too long.

White Moccasin agreed, but he didn't want to deprive his people of their opportunity to celebrate. He looked around.

"Bloody Arm," he said, "you are right, but perhaps we can both let our people sing and dance and also do what we came for."

"Which is . . . ?" Barrett had never been certain why they were heading south.

"Tobacco."

White Moccasin had seen that they were close to the traditional planting grounds, that the soil was right, and that they could conduct the ceremony right there.

And so Barrett/Fawn Eyes/Big Horse/Bloody Arm got to watch the sacred tobacco-planting ceremony. He'd read about it but now he saw it.

The Crow Nation had, from time immemorial, planted tobacco. They had carefully preserved the seed that they found when they first came upon the continent. They believed that as long as they continued to preserve the seed and keep some of the blossoms in their homes, they would preserve their national existence. And as soon as none was to be found, they must pass away from the face of the earth.

In the Crow Nation, all supernatural power was centered in the tobacco-planters, of which there were not many since, besides meeting certain prerequisites, the applicant was required to divest himself of all his wordly possessions and undergo a rigorous ordeal. And though they neither looked nor acted any differently than anyone else, they were credited with the power to control the elements, seasons, animals, and, of course, plants.

Traditionally, in the latter part of April and on the Wind River, beneath the Wind Mountains, the Crow Nation would meet. The ceremony was as follows:

On the first day the women cleared a space of ground, about a half-acre square, of all brush and rubbish. There was singing, drumming, and smoking accompanying the ritual clearing.

On the second day the ground was turned over, using iron instruments or the shoulder blades of buffalo.

On the third day all the married men and women rode off to cut and gather faggots of wood, which they would carry before them on their horses. In bringing the wood back to the cleared area, though, a ritual had to be followed, with exacting requirements.

One woman would ride in first, carrying her faggot of wood. And it was understood that this first woman must be a virtuous woman who had had no illicit connection with any man but her husband—with whom, presumably, such illicit behavior occurred before they became man and wife. Should the woman try to deceive, any man aware of that deception was to step forward and cry, "She is lame," or, in other words, "she is unfit," and the woman was forever disgraced.

This particular disgrace had happened more than once. In fact, the search for a "virtuous" woman had sometimes proved so unrewarding as to nearly cause the suspension of the entire custom. However, they had always succeeded in finding at least one "virtuous" woman, or at least one that no one declared "lame."

But the same problem arose concerning the bearer of the second faggot of wood, a man. He had to be a man who would solemnly swear that he had not committed flagrant incest. It was as hard to find this pillar of virtue as it was to find a virtuous woman. In fact, on one occasion, so anxious were they to locate this upstanding male that they were obliged to employ a member of the American Fur Company to fill the role. And a number of detached observers concluded that unless the Crow people upgraded their moral character, the tobacco-planting rite would soon end.

In any event, that man brought the second bundle and then the rest rode in and laid their faggots down.

The wood was first piled at the four corners of the space. Each pile was then smoked to and celebrated. Then it was spread over the space.

The wood was then burned and the whole area re-hoed and thrashed with willows. The tobacco seed was then mixed with fine earth and ash and spread over the space, and then another willow-thrashing buried the seed.

On the fourth day two things happened. A huge medicine lodge was built in which celebrations and dances and eating started to take place. Second, the medicine man tried to conjure up rain. For the latter effort, the tribe offered up valuables as sacrifices to the clouds. The medicine man hung these valuables up on trees and bushes surrounding the space and then started smoking and praying for rain. If it rained, he got to keep the valuables. If it didn't, he would say the time was not right and the valuables would stay where they were hung.

The rainmaking and the devotions in the medicine lodge usually took about three days, at the end of which time they moved the tent about a half-mile away. The next day they would move it a mile farther, and a mile more the day after that. The idea was that they did not wish the tobacco to think they were running away from it, but rather were so fond of it that they had to drag themselves away.

Four months later they'd return to pull up the plants, from which they'd remove the seeds for storing and the leaves and stems for smoking.

As indicated, this planting was an ancient Crow custom, but it was one that was bound to be changed, if not discontinued, once they'd settled into reservation life.

But White Moccasin and his people were not yet so settled, and they clung to the ceremony, even if what was normally a week-long ceremony was here galloped through in two days.

White Moccasin might have stretched it out longer than two days had he not seen clouds gathering and hastened the process to the rainmaking stage. If he'd read the clouds right, and was successful, they could move out quickly and thereby please Bloody Arm, who was beginning to display impatience.

"Goddamn," cursed Malone. "Who'd have thought it was gonna rain," and he bent his head into the pelting downpour, his campaign hat shielding his face. The entire column rode thusly, thirty soldiers with their heads set on crookedly.

"They'll be gone," said Windy.

"If they went there in the first place," said Matt.

"You can count on it," said Windy. "It's big medicine."

Matt grunted.

Once they'd sallied forth from Outpost Number Nine, they'd headed northwest, first intercepting the North Fork of the Platte and then the North Platte Wagon Road right near Independence Rock, just south of the Rattlesnake Hills.

They followed the road west, for a while paralleling the Sweetwater River as far as St. Mary's Station, where the Bridger Trail branched off.

The Bridger Trail was a way north through the Big Horn Basin to Montana. In 1863, the ageless Jim Bridger had taken emigrants north that way. Matt and his men weren't planning to go as far as Montana, but some fifty miles north of the cutoff, the trail passed near the junction of the Wind and Big Horn Rivers. Tobacco-planting country.

They reached that spot near the end of their second day of riding. The rain had long since stopped. Windy, riding forward, recognized the planting site. And when the column rode up, he stopped them short. "That's hallowed ground," he said, and the men looked at each other.

"We'll go around it, Windy," said Matt. "Lead the way, and look for a good place to bed down."

Windy led the way around and, once beyond the planting site, started looking for a commodious campsite. He thought he saw one up ahead, but when they got there they discovered that the Cheyenne had thought the spot good too.

"Jiminy," breathed Dobbs, staring at the mutilated bodies lying about.

Windy scanned the area and spat. "Cheyenne," he said. "Died quick, too. Crow didn't lose no men."

Matt and the men wondered how he could say that for certain.

"Looks like they celebrated the victory and the tobacco-planting at the same time," Windy concluded.

"Very efficient," remarked Matt. "Is that usual?"

"Nope. Seems like someone or some*thing* might've been hurryin' them. They can celebrate a victory damn near forever, an' tobacco-plantin' usual takes a week or longer."

"Hell, they *had* to be expecting soldiers sooner or later," said Matt, thereby explaining the haste satisfactorily.

Windy picked up a Spencer repeater, of which the breech and firing mechanism were badly damaged. "They picked themselves up some guns too, dozen or more, prob'ly. You hear talk, Matt, about some renegade activity over to South Pass, around Green River, Fort Bridger?" Matt nodded. "Guess this was prob'ly them, or some of them, and they was loaded with high-class weapons."

"Tell me, Windy. This isn't typical of the Crow, is it?"

"Would be if them bodies was Sioux or Blackfoot. But hell, Matt, the Cheyenne are known to be friends with the Sioux."

"So these Crow are not just looking for a place to live free and peacefully."

"No, I still figger that's sure part of it. But remember, Matt, we got ourselves a joker, the renegade that got 'em jumpin' off the reservation, *if* the Captain's right, and I think he is. Besides that, you point a Crow warrior at a Sioux or Blackfoot or someone like that, and all bets are off."

"Well," said Matt, "as long as they stick to killing renegades, I guess it's nothing to get worked up about. And as I told you, I heard they treated that Emigrant Gulch town real kindly."

"White Moccasin ain't dumb, Matt."

"Glad to hear it. Very well, we'll stay around here the night. You ride ahead while it's still light, try to get a fix on where they're headed. Can't be too far ahead. A whole damned village, how fast can they travel?"

twelve

Plenty fast, as it turned out, but not without a bit of good fortune.

Upon leaving the planting site, the Crow had begun to slowly retrace their steps back up the Wind River. They had not gone very far by the time Matt and his men reached the site of the planting and the Cheyenne slaughter. The Crow would probably have been overtaken the next day.

However, they had among them a young warrior who'd drawn his first blood in the attack upon the Cheyenne. He'd danced his head off afterwards, smoked himself sick, and then offered his most valued possession, a bear-tooth necklace, as a sacrifice to the clouds.

When his head cleared, he regretted his impetuous offering. And when the rain began to fall he saw his necklace drop from its branch to be overlooked by White Moccasin as the medicine man collected his booty. So, for the purpose of retrieving his offering and once again reliving the triumphant attack, he returned to the scene.

He watched Windy scout ahead, then followed him back to the American encampment. Then he rode like hell to catch up with the tribe.

Bloody Arm/Barrett thought the soldiers were a pursuit patrol, either from Fort Bridger or Outpost Nine. If from Outpost Nine, those were his erstwhile comrades back there, commanded, he hoped, by one of the less expert second lieutenants. There was no love lost but still, at this point in his transformation, he was reluctant to engage them in combat. Nonetheless, he was a warrior and coming to be accepted as the fiercest warrior, worthy of being called Bloody Arm. Thus he felt compelled to recommend an immediate return to the site and precipitate an attack.

"But they are Americans," argued White Moccasin, as Barrett had hoped he might. The Crow were still in thrall to the white man. Not for much longer, decided Barrett, but for the moment it suited his purposes. "The Sparrowhawk have never killed the Americans," said White Moccasin.

It was not strictly true, but close enough.

"Then we must flee," said Bloody Arm. "They will be upon us with the next sun. We must abandon our village way of traveling and ride with speed."

This was reluctantly agreed upon. The tribe rode farther up the Wind River, into the night, until they came upon a stretch of hard ground. There they sank their travois and nonessentials in the river. Then they all rode into the river's shallows and rode back downstream until they reached a point where a tributary of the Wind joined it from a northerly direction.

They rode up that tributary, staying in the water, until they reached the creek's source, high in the mountains.

It was near dawn by the time they found their way over two small mountain ridges, all part of the Big Horn Mountains, and down to where Owl Creek flowed east to join the Big Horn. Such was the slope at that point, from mountain to plain, that the Big Horn flowed north toward Montana. But although they were headed north, they did not shadow the Big Horn. Instead they crossed the river and, on the other side by some five miles, gained the Bridger Trail.

The Bridger Trail was a good trail, easy to travel, but not heavily traveled, due to the forbidding wilderness through which it ran and rumors of hostile activity. Thus White Moccasin and his people were unimpeded by friend or foe as, the following morning, they rode swiftly north. Even the old women, clinging desperately to horses they had not ridden in many a season, did not slow them.

Matt and his men rode after the Crow the next morning, until they came to a stop on that stretch of hard ground. Matt was baffled and Windy was silent. It took quite some time before evidence of the river dumping—a travois snagged on an underwater rock—was discovered.

"Somehow they found out we were near," concluded Matt, "dumped their gear, and started riding hard and fast. But where?"

"They entered the water right around here," said Windy. "Wouldn't've done that to ride forward, so they did it to ride back down the river."

"Unless," said Matt, smiling, "that's what they *wanted* us to figure out and they really did go up the river...."

"Ain't the kind of thing you'd 'spect from White Moccasin...or even Barrett...."

"Barrett?" repeated Matt, his eyes widening.

"Yep," said Windy. "I been meanin' to mention it. Ever' now and then, past few hours, I been spottin' this one particular track, same track what was made by thet horse Barrett stole...."

Matt stared at him, totally flummoxed.

"Ever hear about a mulatto what became a Crow war chief?" Windy asked.

This was all he needed, thought Matt. "Barrett's a little crazy, he knows he's part colored but *says* he's Indian, wants to be one maybe, runs off, scalps those men in town, and then talks the Crow into leaving the reservation." Matt sighed. "With *him* leading them?"

"White Moccasin and him, maybe. Now it ain't for certain, Matt, all we got to go on is the track, but the timing's right, the *man* is right, and this here little trickery, doublin' back in the water, it's more white than red."

"How about black?" muttered Matt.

Windy shook his head. "All these colors are gettin' confusin'."

"But," said Matt, "you haven't seen any tracks coming *out* of the water, back the way we just came. Did they cross over?"

"Maybe, but I figger they rode down to the first branchin' and then rode up *that* creek. North. I don't figger they got any business goin' south from here."

"Goddammit, Windy, you're guessing. About Barrett—I simply can't believe *that*—and about the Crow."

"Sure," agreed Windy. "Nothin' else I can do. Have you got some better ideas? You want to guess for a while?"

Matt declined, and they followed Windy's guesswork, back down the river and up the first creek north. And four hours later they rested at the source of that creek and triumphantly eyed the many signs of Indian passage—a couple hundred horses can't very well sneak out of a creek.

"This tells me," said Matt, "they're headed for Bridger's trail north. Do we follow them, or have you got a faster way?"

"Follow them," said Windy, biting off a chew of cut plug.

The Crow rode well into each night and rose with the first light to resume their flight. Barrett wondered what the hell he was doing. Some war party, he thought disgustedly, some Bloody Arm. He didn't have to join the Crow in order to ride himself to death.

It seemed to him that White Moccasin enjoyed the running. When they were on the run, White Moccasin was the leader. Come combat, though, and White Moccasin retired to look after the village, his medicine in eclipse. No wonder he didn't care for combat, even though, as Barrett had noted, had he a taste for it, he probably would have been good.

The Bridger Trail swung west to find a fordable spot in the Stinking River, and then it meandered back northeast along the banks of the river until it turned north to pass over the Snow Mountains. Barrett was seeing a lot of the West.

Around noon, the third day of flight, the tribe dashed over the border into Montana. And they were smack dab back in the middle of the Crow reservation.

Barrett was beside himself when he found this out. He rummaged out his packet of maps and found that, sure enough, they'd been riding in a big circle. It was little solace that they were now getting closer to the scene of Custer's destruction at the hands of Sitting Bull, Crazy Horse, and Gall. Those Indians had been Sioux. The only Crow at Little Big Horn had been on *Custer's* side, for crying out loud. No, that wasn't much solace, the nearness of Custer's ghost.

Barrett kept his own counsel, though, and what he suspected turned out to be true: White Moccasin had had his fill of excitement.

White Moccasin was old, weakening, and he'd achieved what *he'd* set out to achieve and he was ready to return to the reservation. Let the Americans have the land. In four months the Sparrowhawk people would jump again and go down and pick their tobacco. But until then, he said, "Let us return to our American friends and the land they have kept for us."

Barrett/Bloody Arm nodded understandingly. And he saw

85

an opportunity. "It is right and good for you to return to the agency, and the Americans, and to keep the village for us. Take with you the older men and women and the youngest children and the horses to get you there.

"The rest of us—Lame Dog, Buffalo Hump, their brother warriors, and myself, Bloody Arm—let us go forth to battle and to find the buffalo"—*that's* a laugh, he thought—"and in several moons, or even several seasons, after such a time of triumph and many coups, we will return to you and you may honor us with dancing and smoking and celebration. . . ."

Well, what could poor White Moccasin say to that. He had declared himself and found the tide running the opposite way; he could see that in the faces of his warriors. So he bade them good hunting, gathered the elderly and the youngest, and led them west, toward the agency. Many of the older men and women, in pain and misery from the long ride, lost no time in dismounting from their horses, content to walk beside them.

Barrett/Bloody Arm was left with a about hundred souls, seventy-five men and twenty-five women. There were many families among them—fathers, mothers, brothers, sisters, lacking only the grandparents and babes. It was still a village, really, full and complete, but now a streamlined, *fighting* village.

"Which way, Bloody Arm?"

"North. To the Blackfoot. To horses and coups."

And so the Crow, now more nearly a war party, streamed north over the Yellowstone River, hellbent for Blackfoot country.

And they were well prepared. They had plenty of guns and ammunition, and although they planned to "borrow" any horse they encountered, they were already well mounted. Each woman had a good horse beneath her and each male, each warrior, no matter how young, rode one horse and led another, his chosen war horse.

Thus they went looking for battle.

They were long gone by the time Matt and his men, riding hard, reached the point on the Bridger Trail where the tribe had split up.

"Looks like some headed back for the reservation," said Windy, squinting at the confusion of sign all around.

"How many?"

"Near half."

"And the rest?"

"North."

"Right, let's go get them and take them back before they get into trouble." Matt laughed. "If it *is* Barrett up ahead, then he's done more riding in the past week or two than he has his whole life. He's probably hurting."

They rode north.

Bloody Arm and his band moved swiftly but carefully. The land was good grass and spread with scrub, cedar, and pine. It was easy traveling, but it was also Blackfoot country. They skirted the Bull Mountains and crossed the Musselshell River. Miles of open country lay before them. And in the distance they saw smoke.

Getting closer, they saw it was a village, almost assuredly Blackfoot, judging from the cant and design of the tipis. Careful scouting determined that it was indeed a Blackfoot village, quiet in the late afternoon heat.

"How many?" asked Bloody Arm.

"Near as many men as us," replied the scout.

A good battle, thought Barrett, but he was surprised by his warriors' unhappy countenances. Then he remembered that the Indians did not care for even battles, that they liked to over-whelm lesser foes and thereby minimize the chances of taking any losses themselves.

"Good, good," declared Bloody Arm, getting the jump on his dispirited companion. "They match us in numbers, *if* they are ready, but they are not. They sleep. After our first assault there will be but a handful remaining to withstand our warriors. Come, let us plan the attack."

Thus he hooked them before they had a chance to object. He threw his chest out and strutted about in eager anticipation, shaming them into compliance. And plans were laid.

And it worked out much as Bloody Arm said it would. Half of the Crow warriors, with Barrett in the lead, moved close on foot, to the very edge of the Blackfoot village. The rest of the warriors, some thirty to forty, stayed farther back, mounted, hidden in a draw. They would come at the first cry, the first shot, and would be a second wave sweeping irresistibly through and devastating those trying to retreat or escape.

And that's the way it happened. Again Bloody Arm drew

first blood, and not reluctantly, because his "father," having departed with White Moccasin, was not going to have to give anything away.

Many coups were counted and scalps collected, warm and dripping with red blood.

As was the Crow custom, they spared the women and children, gathering the best looking of the younger women and the strongest of the boys to mix with their own people. However, there was another Crow custom that here came into play.

Three of the Crow attackers had died in the initial assault, and now their surviving family members mourned their deaths, which they did by moaning and wailing in the most frightful manner (to Barrett's inexperienced ear) and by chopping off parts of their fingers and darkening their faces with blood. Barrett almost vomited; there seemed to be fingers dropping all over the place.

This couldn't go on forever, thought Barrett, but apparently it could. The wailing and bloodletting went into and through the night and was still going on the next day.

Then he recalled, from his readings in the Culbertson manuscripts, tales of Indian mourners known to have wandered the mountains for years, unwashed, black with dried blood, fingers missing, filthily robed, wailing....

Bloody Arm/Barrett was at his wits' end. He learned from Lame Dog that only a magnificent victory, losing no lives and counting many coups, could stop the wailing.

Barrett immediately formed a war party and led them from the Blackfoot village in desperate search of prey.

thirteen

Barrett/Bloody Arm and his band of twelve, which included Lame Dog, Spotted Elk, and Buffalo Hump, ranged far in search of the necessary coups. They traveled north, crossing Yellow Water Creek, McDonald's Creek, Box Elder Creek, Wood Creek, Blood Creek, Cat Creek. . . .

They found some white settlements, which they avoided, but no Blackfoot, nor any other tribe.

Black Butte, Haystack Butte, and Dovetail Butte watched over them from the west. Little Belt Mountain was dead ahead, and beyond it, the Missouri.

The Crow had once lived along the Missouri, a sedentary, horticultural tribe. That was before they split from the Hidatsas, or Gros Ventres, to become the nomadic, mountain-ranging, hunting and meat-eating Absaroka (or Crow, as the Sioux took to calling them in derision).

But the Missouri was far enough. Too far, in fact. They turned around. Perhaps the wailing would be over by the time they got back, the cutting and bleeding done with.

On the way south, Barrett/Bloody Arm decided to stop at one of the small white settlements, a place that might as well have been called a large ranch.

Various activities were performed there. Sheep and cattle and goats and pigs were raised, grain and corn were grown in small amounts, trappers and hunters worked out of it, as did some miners, though the big strikes were to the west and south in Montana's Rockies. The settlement's stable population was generally about twenty, three-quarters of which were adults, the rest youngsters of varying ages.

Bloody Arm and his men rode quietly into the settlement. Though they made the sign of peace and behaved appropriately, they were adorned with warpaint. Small wonder that the settlement's inhabitants were a trifle edgy.

A balding man advanced on them, trailed by two younger men. All carried rifles.

"Do you speak English?"

Barrett nodded.

"What do you want?"

"We come in peace," said Barrett/Bloody Arm, whose eyes had spied a truly beautiful young woman, peering fearfully from one of the buildings. "We will trade you a horse for some food and grain." Each warrior had his war horse, they could spare one. Or two, even.

"We don't need no Injun horses," sneered one of the young men.

"But perhaps you could spare some food and grain anyway," said Barrett stonily; the young man reminded him of Private Popper.

"'Perhaps,' huh," said the balding older man. "You talk the language pretty good." He stared hard at Barrett. "You don't look like no Injun."

"But I am. We are Absaroka. Sparrowhawk."

"Never heard of yuh. Blackfoot I know—damned horse thieves—an' Assiniboines an' Crow, them I know, but I never heard of you 'hawk' people."

Barrett despaired of explaining further. "The Blackfoot," said Barrett, "do you know where we might find them?"

"Ain't been none around here, not fer a hunnert miles thataway." He pointed west. "Whaddaya want them fer, anyway?"

"We wish to kill them," said Barrett, and he smiled winningly through his war paint, not realizing how grotesque it looked.

The girl still watched curiously as the men stared, astounded. Then one of the younger men stepped closer to eye Barrett's rifle, which hung by his leg. "Looks like a repeater. Hell, what's a bloody Injun doin' with a nice piece like that?"

Barrett kept silent, though he stiffened.

The young man that reminded Barrett of Popper looked around. "Hell, they *all* got nice pieces," he said. Then, eyeing

90

Barrett's again: "Like to own thet one myself." Barrett saw the young man's hand hover close to a holstered gun, even though he already held a rifle. "Looks newer'n mine." And it was. The young man obviously paid more attention to his pistols than his rifle.

"Mebbe he'll trade, Josh," said the older man.

More people had begun to come from the buildings, satisfied that there was no danger.

"Shit, ain't gonna trade with no Injun. Soon's trade with them as trade with a nigger."

Barrett, already tense, fought to control himself. But his brain started to boil.

"Hell," said the other young man, "take it from 'im, Josh."

Josh turned quickly and, with a grin or grimace, grabbed for the rifle.

Barrett's horse shied, backing.

"*Hold still,* Injun," shouted the other young man, waving his rifle as a general threat.

A cry issued from Barrett/Bloody Arm as he kicked his mount into a forward lunge. One arm raised his hatchet high while his other hand snatched for the Scoff stuck deep in the waistband of his leggings.

The balding man and the other younger man fell back before the lunging horse as the hatchet fell to bury itself in Josh's head. Then Barrett's Scoff was thundering, first nailing the younger man, whose rifle fired harmlessly skyward, and then the balding man, catching him with a look of horror on his face.

Then Barrett's band opened fire. . . .

The return of Bloody Arm and his men to the Crow encampment was the occasion of great rejoicing. They brought with them ten scalps and had lost none of their own party, though two had been wounded.

The celebration was shortlived, however. It was interrupted when the discovery was made that the scalps were from white men (their prisoners were obviously white, but they were not out in front of the triumphal procession).

"No, hear me," shouted Bloody Arm. "They, as much as the Sioux and Blackfoot, have become our enemies. The Americans have taken our land, our horses, our customs, our pride. It is they who have tried to take our manhood, not the Sioux, not the Blackfoot. Why should we respect their lives when they do not respect ours?"

Most of the Crow were trapped in ambivalence. Even Barrett's war party had done their killing with extreme misgiving. The Americans were traditionally their friends. And if *they* had misgivings, it was no surprise that the rest of the Crow had even more.

But Barrett's words were undeniably true. If Lame Dog himself had not said as much, he'd thought it.

And White Moccasin, their revered medicine man, was not there to condemn the action.

No, Barrett/Bloody Arm carried the day, at least to some degree. Many of the Crow, though, too imbued with tradition, found they could not follow a leader who flouted those old traditions.

So it was that Barrett/Bloody Arm's band was reduced by more than half. Staying with him were many of the warriors and the two young white women and the boy who had been taken from the settlement. But folding their tents and renouncing their warlike ways were Waterfly, Leaf That Cries, some of the older warriors, and all the women. But added to that group were several white women and two white children who had also been taken from the settlement. They all rode off southwesterly, heading slowly in the general direction of the agency. They were going home, or back to what they would finally accept as home.

Bloody Arm and his men watched them go. Barrett/Bloody Arm feigned sadness, but he did not feel it. He finally had a sleek, well-conditioned, blooded war party at his disposal, larger than an army platoon and committed to his warlike ways, to his violent dream.

"I take a new name," he announced, "to go with Bloody Arm. It is Medicine Calf. It is a name that will strike fear into all we encounter and that will lead us to triumph after triumph."

And he led them west.

The next day, Matt Kincaid and his saddle-weary combat patrol arrived at the scene of the Blackfoot massacre. He shook his head, grimacing.

The rest of the patrol edged their horses closer, encircling the encampment, looking it over with interest.

"Take a reading, Windy," Matt said. "We'll pull back a ways. Stinks too bad."

Half an hour later, Windy came riding upwind from the encampment, to where Matt waited with the patrol.

"Big doin's, Matt. They ain't been gone that long. They wiped out the village, all right. But they wasn't so lucky this time. Lost a few themselves. That calls for a whole lot of wailin' and mournin', and usually don't end till someone goes out and scores a big victory and comes back safe and with coups. That makes everything all right and they go about their business. So I figger, and the tracks agree, that some went north and came back with scalps. But then it appears they split up. A lot went thataway"—he pointed southwest—"and the rest thataway. The bigger bunch went southwest."

"Toward the reservation."

"Maybe so."

"Why?"

Windy shrugged mysteriously.

"So we should probably follow the ones that went straight west. They're probably still up to no good. Let's—"

"Matt, I think we better go find where they got their scalps."

"C'mon, Windy, we're not here to keep track of how many hostiles they kill. We're out to *catch* 'em."

"Matt. We better."

Matt rarely, if ever, argued with Windy, who rarely said more than he had to, and was rarely wrong.

Matt mounted his patrol up and led them off. Their course took them back through the Blackfoot village.

"*Gott im Himmel!*" squawked Holzer, partway through the village.

Matt, eyes trained on the horizon, halted the column upon hearing the exclamation and looked back.

Holzer stared down, then leaped from his horse. He picked something up from the ground. He held it up. "*Was ist . . . ?*" he began, though he knew damned well what it was.

"It's a finger, Wolfie," Windy called back, "or a piece of one."

Wolfgang Holzer dropped the joint as if it were still alive.

"When they mourn the dead," explained Windy, "they cut off fingers. Look around, they're all over."

The men started staring at the ground, wide-eyed, horrified

as they came to realize that the ground was positively littered with pieces of fingers.

Windy laughed, but Matt decided to get the column moving again as quickly as possible.

fourteen _____

Back at Outpost Number Nine boredom reigned. Most of Easy wished they'd gotten to go along with Lieutenant Kincaid. A nice long ride chasing some friendly Crow, stopping off in some towns, maybe meeting some new gals . . . all sorts of good things. Catch the Crow, take 'em back, and then settle in for a long, drunken ride home. That was the good life.

Some men, though, weren't all that bored. There was still occasional thieving, and Weasel Gillies was steering clear of shadows. Save one particular shadow, little Billy.

"Hell, Weasel, it's *gotta* be her. I tell yuh, I was hid in there, and after Malone 'n' Dobbs left, she jes' stood there lookin' aroun'."

"That's 'cause she's a whoor, that's why. Thet blond bitch is jes' lookin' aroun' figgerin' which bed she'd like to share. And now, with ol' Plowright out chasin' hostiles, she's about fit t' be tied. Hell, I'm prob'ly the only man she hasn't made a pass at."

"Ain't made a pass at me," said Billy.

"Don't go gettin' yerself any big ideas," snorted Weasel.

Corporal Medford had big ideas too, fervid besides, but of a strictly puritanical nature. He couldn't believe the slime this man's army was taking on. All they could think about was *women*, and the things they could *do* with women. Disgusting!

Of course, it could be said—and *was* said—that Medford spent so much time sniffing around for dirt that he had to be pretty dirty himself. Which was true. But Medford couldn't

95

come anywhere near seeing that, much less admitting his own sexuality. That was a closed part of his mind. And in that respect he resembled Sergeant Plowright.

Good man, Plowright, decided Medford. Though married, still good. He understood that Plowright kept his wife at a proper distance, indulging his lowest appetites only when appearances, or his less pure wife, demanded.

Medford sat in the afternoon mess over a cup of coffee. Coffee was always available, twenty-four hours a day, and if you treated Dutch or his cooks right—extra tobacco rations, stuff like that—food was available too. At the moment he was waiting for a thin slice (they had to make it stretch) of fresh beef between a couple of slabs of Dutch's good sourdough.

When the hand touched his shoulder, his head snapped around guiltily, almost snapping off his shoulders and dousing the hand with spittle.

Clara Plowright smiled down at him. "What are you doing, Corporal? Got nothing to do?"

He had something to do, all right—eat—but he sure didn't want her watching him doing it. Watching and knowing he was getting special favors. "Coffee, that's all." He got up and tried to get her moving out the mess door. "Bet you miss ol' Ernest something awful," he said.

"Ernie? Blowhard?" She laughed gaily. "Whatever for? Goodness, when I've got men like *you* . . . She reached out and fingered a button on his shirt. "You ought to keep this buttoned. Don't want anyone getting the wrong idea." The smile she gave him was loaded with the "wrong idea."

Medford backed off suddenly, slapping at her hand and yelping, "Don't you touch me." His face got ugly and he snarled, "I know your kind, I know what you're after, you're just . . . *filth.*"

She was stunned and, for then and a good while afterwards, hurt. She was not an evil woman, a bitch or a whore, just a healthily lusty and damnably frustrated thing who wasn't all that bright. She'd gone into the marriage with her eyes open. Yet she actually saw little, understood less, and lacked the intelligence to handle the situation that developed. When Ernest ignored her, she assumed he'd also ignore her seeking pleasure elsewhere, ignore if not approve. And she did seek it obviously.

The trouble was, it wasn't easy to find. Everyone seemed

determined to treat her as a "married lady." Untouchable. It made her angry and she wanted to strike back. So she stole from them, not because she needed the various items, but to hurt.

She retreated now from the mess and, blistering, slipped into the barracks. "Sergeant Chubb," she called, knowing Chubb was many miles away, with darling Ernest. "Sergeant Chubb," she called again.

No response, no noise of any kind; the place was empty.

She slipped over to the bunk closest to her. She hoped that it belonged to that Corporal Medford, but she really didn't care that much.

The men were keeping their things better hidden these days, but she managed to dig out a wallet. It was empty, but made of good leather with fancy carving. She tucked it down her dress and quickly left the barracks, going to the first man she saw outside and asking him where Sergeant Chubb was, since he wasn't in his room.

"No ma'am, Sergeant Chubb's out in the field. Been gone a while now."

"Oh, pshaw."

Inside the barracks, Weasel Gillies and Billy stepped from behind the suffocating buffalo coats where they'd been hiding.

"Now we can tell 'em," said Billy.

"Tell 'em? Tell 'em *what?* They ain't gonna believe *me.* My word agin hers? Nossirree, I've gotta *show* 'em. Now you get out there, Billy, get aholt of that whoor an' don't let her get away, don't let her ditch thet wallet. I'm gonna go round up my *comrades* and get 'em back here. You wait fer my signal and then bring 'er in."

They both went out different doors, Billy emerging and saying, "Hey, there, Miz Plowright, you got time to tell me somethin'?"

Clara Plowright stared at Billy. "Tell you what, Billy?"

"You been to a big city, right? Well . . ."

Twenty minutes later—Clara talking her head off the whole time about the "big city," namely St. Louis—Billy got the high sign from Weasel and said, "Miz Plowright, 'scuse me breakin' in, but . . . could you come into the barracks wi' me? I got somethin' t' show yuh."

Good Lord, she thought, he's not going to whip down his pants, is he? Still, as often as not, little men had giant-sized peckers. Wonder if he's old enough to get it up? "Why, I'd be delighted, Billy," she said, and followed him inside.

Where she encountered not only Billy's buddy, Weasel, but also Privates Moore, Standifer, the giant Trouble Thompson, Beasley and Buford Champlain, a tried-but-unconvicted rapist from Maryland.

"Well," declared Clara brightly, "what have we here?"

Clara had clean forgotten about the wallet stuffed down her bodice, the outline of which was clear to a sharp eye, and what "we had" were five highly irritable privates who had each lost an article or two over the past few weeks. Champlain was the owner of the wallet.

"All right, Weasel, yer ass is on the line," growled Moore.

Weasel stepped forward quickly. Clara shied away, but before she could get far, Weasel was upon her, stuffing his hand down her bodice.

For a giddy moment he realized he'd never felt tits like that, but he kept his mind on business and found and extracted the wallet. He tossed it to Champlain, who already knew that it was missing.

Champlain caught the wallet in the air and casually tossed it behind him, his eyes hot and fastened on Clara.

Dread enveloped Clara, and her skin grew clammy.

"What're we gonna do?" wondered Thompson.

"Do?" said Champlain, stepping toward Clara, who was frozen in place. He took Clara by the neckline of her bodice and pulled gently. "Come on in here, little lady. We're gonna ad-minister some old-time barracks justice."

"Aw, shit, Buford, we cain't beat 'er up."

"But there ain't nothin' wrong with the *ee*-quivalent, is there?" Buford continued to gently pull Clara, who moved slowly.

"Whaddaya mean?"

"Well, *hell*, you seen this little lady, if you can call her that. She's been suckin' up t' everythin' what wears pants 'round here. 'Bout time we gave her what she's been askin' fer."

"Hey. That's Plowright's wife."

"And about time Plowright knew what he's got, right? Don't we owe our buddy Plowright that? Straighten him out?"

"Maybe we oughta jes' turn her in," ventured Weasel.

"S'prised at you, Weasel," said Champlain. "I figgered you'd go first. You kinda got it comin', you been takin' all the shit from ev'body."

"The first *what*?" demanded Clara, suddenly regaining her senses and standing fast.

"Goddammit, *move!*" shouted Champlain, jerking at her bodice.

The bodice tore and Clara's tits came popping out, big and bouncy and juicy as a couple of good-sized grapefruits. But a hell of a lot sweeter, thought Champlain.

Clara started to try to cover herself, but then stopped. Her breath was short and she felt her sex dampening.

"Christ, this damn whoor *wants* it," cried Champlain, and he stepped forward and started ripping the rest of Clara's clothes off. "Goddammit, Weasel, git yer pants down."

For a moment, Weasel was indecisive, during which interval Billy cried, "I'm here too, I'm Weasel's buddy!" but then Weasel thought, what the hell, I'll never get another chance like this.

Champlain had dropped Clara to the floor and spread her legs. The other men, in various stages of readiness, stared down at the golden mound of her sex. Clara's eyes were open and empty and fixed on the ceiling. She couldn't stand the idea of eye contact. But she did wish it would start.

What could she do? she asked herself. She was helpless. All these strong men, these brutes...

Then Weasel clambered onto her and went into her. She reflected that she'd been right about small men often being big where it counted.

She suddenly felt good and began to go with the feeling.

Weasel finished faster than he wanted to, and then found he had only the unappetizing sight of Champlain's heaving, pimply ass to look at. Billy stood to the side, the rope that held up his trousers untied. He was ready.

It ain't right, thought Weasel, now that he'd gotten his. It's gonna ruin everything for her and that dumb Plowright bastard. It oughta be stopped.

You gonna stop it? he asked himself.

Hell no.

You gonna run to the orderly room and report it?

Again, hell no. My life wouldn't be worth shit.

Then what're you gonna do?

I'm gonna get careless and blab to the wrong person, and *he's* gonna run to the orderly room.

And so Weasel slipped from the barracks and went looking for Corporal Medford. He found him still in the mess, feeding his face. Weasel flopped down beside him. Medford stared at him, recoiling in horror; Weasel was probably his least favorite soldier, degeneracy incarnate.

"Jeez, Corp, you wanna get in on somethin' *good*, you better move yo' ass fast. I don' figger she's gonna last much longer."

Medford scowled. "Just what are you babbling about, Private?" he enunciated slowly.

Thirty seconds later, though, there was nothing slow about him as he burst from the mess and dashed across the parade to the orderly room, shouting all the way.

Private Tompkins, walking guard up top, was so unnerved that he almost shot Medford down, for a moment thinking that, for variety, Mr. Lo was attacking from *inside* the outpost. Tompkins was a very nervous sort.

By the time Tompkins' breathing had returned to normal, Medford was back out of the orderly room, leading a stampede across the parade. In the stampede were Sergeant Cohen and Lieutenants Allison and Smaldoon. Captain Conway had come to the door of the orderly room and was watching. Now he spoke, and Bradshaw appeared and ran toward the dependent housing. Conway himself strode toward his own quarters.

The stampede entered the barracks, and by the time Cohen and Smaldoon reappeared, marching the "rapists" ahead of them, both Flora Conway and Maggie Cohen were bearing down on the barracks. Mr. Allison had stayed behind to comfort the poor, ravished Clara Plowright, who, Allison noted calmly, was fighting to keep a grin off her face.

Champlain, marching stiffly, suddenly twisted his head. "Weasel!" he roared toward Private Gillies, who'd stuck his head out of the mess. "Did you let on to thet bastard Medford?"

"I didn't know," whined Weasel, "I jes' thought he might be innerested. You know, might wanta—"

Medford, hearing the exchange, grew red with outrage.

"The hell you didn't," called bullet-headed, Moore, laughing nonetheless. "Don' worry, though, we all got ours . . . Billy too."

Weasel smiled. It was working out fine.

"Gillies!" roared Cohen. "Get your ass over here!"

No, it wasn't.

It took quite a while to unravel everything. Initially, of course, the men were accused of the grossest kind of rape.

"But there's somethin' y' gotta unnerstan', Sarge," said Weasel, "an' Captain, sir," he added, glancing at Conway. "That effin' whoor's a thief. I caught her, *we* caught her, red-handed. We figgered she needed punishin', but what were we s'posed to do, beat her up?"

"You've got proof?" asked Cohen, momentarily taken aback.

"Goddamn right we had proof, Sarge, an' we're all witnesses. An' if you'll check Blowhard's quarters, you'll prob'ly find every last missin' thing."

Captain Conway, listening, agreed that put matters in a different light, but he let Cohen continue to do the talking.

"You should have turned her in."

"Not me, Sarge. You're lookin' at a man thet damn near got killed 'cause o' her. I pay my debts, Sarge. An' we had plenty good reason." Gillies, at that moment, looked especially righteous. Champlain, beginning to see himself as a hero, forgave Weasel his ratting. "Besides," said Weasel, "jes' about everyone knows the bitch is a whoor."

"I don't think Clara Plowright's a whore," said Captain Conway. "Do you, Sergeant?"

Cohen was sensible but old-fashioned, and wasn't sure. "I don't think Maggie'd call her that," he said.

Conway smiled. "Nor, I venture to say, would Flora." A couple of hours later, Captain Conway had personally interviewed everyone who might possibly shed any light on the matter, which meant he'd interviewed damn near everyone on the post.

"All right, Sergeant, these are the facts. The men *did* violate Clara Plowright. She was a consistent and apparently resourceful thief, for what reason God only knows, though I have my suspicions. She had also flaunted herself and made known her carnal desires to almost every man on the post. And Mr. Allison is willing to swear that she enjoyed the, uh, violation. So, it's a matter demanding the wisdom and judgment of Solomon, but it's only going to get the mundane and pragmatic wisdom of

Conway. Extreme measures in the way of punishment are not, to my mind, warranted. But neither can it be condoned, or the censure misinterpreted.

"I want those men put on hard labor, the hardest you can find, for two months. Time off to eat, time off to sleep, one afternoon a week off for whatever, and that's it. Work their bloody asses off. And that's exclusive of any combat requirements. Hell, maybe they'll get lucky, and go out after Mr. Lo and get themselves blown away...

"Clara goes to Flora and Maggie for care and for, ummm, companionship, shall we say, and nowhere else. I don't want her loose at all.

"You'll cut transfer papers for Sergeant Plowright. We'll have them approved. Tell 'em we've got all the sergeants we need. When Plowright gets back, he'll hardly have time to slow down before he's on his way back out, along with Clara, who I assume will keep her mouth shut."

"What if Sergeant Plowright hears about it anyway, sir, and wants blood? And believe me, sir, he'll want blood."

"Well, then, Sergeant," said Captain Conway quietly, "I guess we'll just have to wait until we see the whites of his eyes."

"It was awful, Maggie. First they accused me of *stealing*...and then...oh, God, it was awful. But what could I do?"

That was right at the start. Clara had tried to work up some tears but had only managed to get misty-eyed.

Maggie had not suggested she might have screamed.

Then came word that the stolen items had indeed been found in the Plowright quarters.

"*I* didn't take them," declared Clara. "I don't know *how* they got there. Maybe...do you think maybe Sergeant Plowright...?"

Maggie treated it as a wild and desperate suggestion.

Later, Flora and Maggie got together and agreed that Clara was not really bad, just the victim of a preposterous mismatch, and also that the situation defied any solution other than Warner Conway's.

Clara couldn't understand why she couldn't leave her quarters.

And finally she inquired softly, "Those men, they won't be punished badly, will they?"

fifteen

Matt Kincaid and his patrol rode for several hours. They crossed Yellow Water Creek, and kept their eyes peeled for signs of Indian encampments where, most likely, the Crow had collected the coups that had canceled their own.

The men were tired, and sagged in their saddles.

They came to a point where the sign leading north diverged from that of the returning band.

"Must have found something off that way," said Windy, and they rode off in that direction.

The land was rolling prairie, slowly descending in elevation toward the east.

Around a bend, then around a stand of cedar and scrub, the settlement came into view. It looked peaceful from a distance, except that various domestic animals seemed to be running around free. And there wasn't any sign of human life.

"All out workin', maybe," said Windy.

"Let's hope so," said Matt.

The closer they got, the faster they drove their mounts, as they began to discern bodies scattered about.

They swept into the settlement in a state of horror and outrage. Some eight bodies lay about in full view, cleanly shot, most of them, but their heads bloody.

The men hit the ground running, guns out. But all they found were seven more victims, inside the housing. The jobs done on them, at close quarters, had been messier.

Most of the bodies belonged to men of varying ages. There were a few younger women among the victims, but mistakes might have been made; the Crow didn't usually slaughter women. And no children. They thanked God for that. If the raiders had been Sioux, they'd likely have found babes with their heads smashed pulpy.

"You guessed," said Matt to Windy, almost an accusation.

"Figgered the coups might have made the Crow split up. An' if they did, it might've been because the victims were white. Worth seein'."

Before Matt, his breath still short and his stomach knotting, could decide what to do, two women appeared. Old women, and clearly women. The Crow had seen them trying to hide and had let them go.

From them, Matt got a description of the attack. Somewhat biased, of course, but Matt took that into consideration. There'd been provocation, Matt understood, but not nearly enough to bring about this kind of slaughter—just a couple of dumb white boys opening their stupid mouths.

But that final exchange, according to the old woman, had involved a rifle and had contained contemptuous references to "Injuns" and "niggers." Matt had forgotten all about Barrett, but now it came back. Those words might have set the match to the powder keg. Maybe they *were* dealing with Barrett, after all, the crazy, sensitive black-*cum*-red man. Damn. An intuitive certainty that they were chasing Barrett began to grow.

"And one of them, the leader," added one of the old women, "was called Bloody Arm. He called himself that."

"In *English*?"

Just then Windy came up and said, "Found a hell of a funny thing out back, Matt."

Matt regarded him gloomily.

"A lot of animals have been killed and skinned. Some meat taken, of course, but the skins, they been stretched to dry and each one's got 'JB' cut in it."

"Now what the hell would he do that for?" Matt mumbled to himself, and then he just shook his head helplessly.

Matt then sent a soldier hightailing south for the nearest fort, Fort Tullock, on the far side of the Yellowstone, to let them know what had happened: that the Crow reservation-jumpers were now a war party hitting whites as well as other tribes, that they were headed west, probably along the Musselshell River, and that although Matt was giving immediate chase, Forts Howe and Ellis had best be alerted. The message also told of the Crow split.

Matt watched the rider vanish around the far bend and then he organized burial parties. "Just dig 'em deep enough to keep them hidden safely. And do it fast—we've got to move." And to underscore the urgency, both Matt and Windy grabbed shovels and helped with the digging.

A half-hour later they were ready.

"What'll we do with the old women?" inquired Sergeant Chubb.

Matt cursed under his breath.

"We'll be all right, Cap'n," croaked one old lady. "You just go catch those murderin' bastards."

"Besides," said the other old lady, "we ain't budgin'. This was our home and it still is. Iffen we leave, someone might take it. An' iffen you catch up to them killers, you might get the girls back, an' the little boys. They gotta have a home to come back to."

A couple of tough old biddies, thought Matt, even though their eyes looked empty. "All right, then, we'll get word out that you're here. Someone'll come."

And with that, he signaled the patrol into motion and they swarmed out of the settlement and back southward.

When they reached the site of the Blackfoot slaughter, their horses hardly broke stride as they swung west.

White Moccasin left his people where their village had been, by Big Boulder River, and rode on to the agency.

The agent emerged to stare at him. News had just come over the telegraph wire.

"We have returned," said White Moccasin, "to stay. But we have nothing. We need food and canvas for tipis, and horses and milk cows and tools to dig in the earth, and we need young men to do the work and to be police, for our people will now become white . . ."

The agent continued to stare. "You're *all* back?"

"No," White Moccasin replied sorrowfully, "just the elders and the youngest. The warriors still roam free, with the antelope

105

and other wild things, but they will return soon, for . . . for no more things run free. . . ."

The agent's shoulders slumped. He eyed White Moccasin sadly. The chief, even at his advanced age, looked good in his buckskin shirt and leggings, appropriated from the Cheyenne, and he had a bright, healthy gaze, and his hair was standing up in front, four inches high, in the proud Crow manner. The agent would have to find him some old cotton trousers and a shirt—ill-fitting, no doubt.

"Return to your village, White Moccasin. I will send someone."

White Moccasin turned away, still looking proud. But so beaten was he, so complete was his real defeat, that when, several weeks later, Chief Joseph and the Nez Perce, closely pursued by General Howard, came through and sought help, the Crow did refuse. And not only refused their brethren, but told them that the Crow would be helping General Howard.

A combined force from Forts Sarpy and Tullock intercepted Waterfly, Leaf That Cries, and some sixty-odd members of the tribe near Willow Creek, as the band was about to cross the Yellowstone and enter the reservation.

They did, in fact, cross, but under army guard and after the white women and children had been taken from them.

The women and children were returned, eventually, to the two old women and that settlement, which had been restocked with more members of the same large clan, summoned by the two old matriarchs.

Only one young boy and two women of tender years had yet to be accounted for.

And, finally, it was John "Weasel" Gillies' half-day off. He felt broken in fifty pieces by the hard labor to which Sergeant Cohen had been subjecting him and the others.

Yet he'd mounted a horse and ridden nearly fifty miles to the town of Morgan's Hollow. Little Billy Caber lived there somewhere. Gillies hadn't seen the boy since he'd been practically whipped off the post and told never to return.

It didn't take Gillies long to track down the Cabers. He knew Bull Caber, the father, was a drinker, so he went from saloon to saloon until he found him. But the man was drunk, naturally, and mean, and Billy wasn't there. Eventually, judicious inquiry told Weasel where the Cabers lived.

The Caber home was above a saloon, but not the one Bull Caber was holed up in. The door was opened by Billy, who might have been glad to see him but didn't show it.

Behind Billy, a spectral figure in white appeared, then vanished. "That's my ma," said Billy, not inviting him in. But Weasel entered anyway.

He looked over the small, poorly furnished apartment, all the while discreetly eyeing the slight, pale woman whose thin white robe reminded Weasel of an empty, crumpled envelope. Rosy spots that weren't rouge glowed on each cheek. Red, watery eyes swam to him and tried to focus. She'd been a pretty woman once. Now she looked like she was dying.

"Pa brung 'er here to make her well," said Billy.

Should've brung 'er a thousand miles south o' here, thought Weasel.

"Ma don't like it so much, but Pa..."

The woman reached out then and took a piece of Billy's flesh between her fingers and pinched until he cried out. She smiled weakly then, her eyes sagging open, and said, "There, there, Billy. You an' me, we're meant for pain."

Billy stared at her with tears in his eyes—but fear in his posture.

It was the damnedest relationship Weasel had ever seen; Mrs. Caber made his own mama seem a dream by comparison.

Footsteps thudded on the stairs, and moments later Bull Caber staggered in. Millicent Caber struggled to her feet, smiling a welcome.

Bull Caber glared at her, condemning her weakness, and then fetched Billy a wild, backhanded smack. "Help yer goddamn mother!" he bellowed.

Weasel felt anger but Bull Caber, though short, was named appropriately and was bigger than Weasel. Besides, Weasel hadn't gotten a real good line yet on how Billy felt about them, deep down. He found Bull Caber's red eyes fastened on him. "Who the hell's this?" demanded Bull.

Before either Billy or Weasel could answer, though, a shout came from down below somewhere:

"Hey, Bull! Git aholt o' yer goddamn rifle. Injuns on the warpath. We're gonna go get us some."

Weasel frowned, watching Bull Caber lurch toward the corner of the room, and decided he'd best be getting back to the post. It'll die down soon, Billy," he said to the small boy. "You come see me, y' hear?" And then Weasel was gone.

sixteen _____

Weasel rode as hard as he could for Outpost Number Nine. If Indians, or 'Mr. Lo,' as he was learning to call them, were on the warpath, then Sergeant Cohen would be too, even though Weasel legitimately had the afternoon off. He thought of the five other "rapists." They'd dragged their weary bones as far as their bunks and no farther. Sure as anything, as soon as the alarm sounded they'd be falling out lickety-split, brown-nosing for all they were worth.

Weasel was tougher than they were, and they knew it. But that didn't cause him to feel any particular pride or contempt. It was just a fact, that was all. Christ, when he was twelve, he'd worked his tiny butt raw in a traveling carny, pulling a hell of a lot more than his own weight, setting up and striking. And when he was fourteen, he'd worked as a sandhog, crawling in where others couldn't and working fourteen-hour shifts.

Hell, these men didn't know what work was. Sure, he was aching, but he wasn't tired. And he could ride. The fifty miles flew by. And the horse enjoyed it; having Gillies up top was like carrying nothing at all.

He was about a quarter-mile from the outpost when dust kicked up nearby, followed by the crack of a distant shot. What the hell?

He rode closer, but slowly and carefully. He could see a lot of activity around the lookout tower, figures moving. He hoped the place hadn't been taken over by Indians.

"Halt!"

He drew up.

"Advance and be recognized."

He moved his horse forward slowly, trying to puzzle it out. It didn't sound like an Indian. Sounded like—

Then he heard another voice.

"Goddammit, Tompkins, what the hell're you doin'? That's *Weasel*."

Tompkins. He might have known. And then he saw someone grabbing for Tompkins' rifle.

Private Gillies rode in the opened gate, half expecting to find a patrol mounted and ready to charge out and do battle. He didn't, though. He didn't see a damn thing except Sergeant Cohen and Captain Conway standing in front of the orderly room, staring angrily across the parade to where Tompkins was making excuses to the sergeant of the guard.

Gillies thought he'd check in with Cohen.

"What're you doing back, Private? You had the afternoon off."

"Heard Mr. Lo was on the warpath, Sarge. Figgered I'd better get back."

"Where'd you hear that?"

"Town . . . over to Morgan's Hollow, actually."

Cohen's eyebrows rose, but he didn't comment on the obvious purpose of Gillies' visit. He did say, though, "On the warpath, huh? Up in central Montana there's a bunch makin' trouble, but . . ." He turned to Warner Conway. "Don't sound good, sir. Sounds like the news of Matt's bunch has got down here already. What with those boys scalped in town, we may be in for some trouble." He scowled. "And what do you think of the word Matt sent down about Private Barrett, Crow war chief? You settin' any store by that, sir? Think he was the one that scalped those jaspers in town?"

Conway didn't like thinking about it, not any of it. The corners of his mouth pulled down. It sounded like there might be some "police action" in the offing, but that would be it, nothing glorious, nothing that earned promotions. The muscles in his jaw worked. As for the likelihood that Private Barrett had gone totally insane and transformed himself into a bloodthirsty Crow war chief . . .

Captain Conway sighed, then growled, "Make sure the men are ready, Sergeant. We may have to move out fast. Light gear, nothing more. "And make sure Mister Price is ready."

109

He smiled a thin, cold smile. "Do it gently, though."

"You mean I can't discharge my weapon into his door?"

Gillies, who'd already gotten an earful, was grinning.

"What are you grinning at, soldier?" barked Cohen. "You get about your business, *fast*, or I'll find you some. And you be ready, you especially. I figure we might get you scalped in the next few days."

Gillies lit his horse out for the stables. Damn, a man couldn't even *grin* around this effin' place.

Nearing the stables, he almost crashed into Moore and Champlain, who were leading horses out of the stables. Apparently they'd recovered enough to make a gesture toward town. Weasel skidded his horse to a stop. "Jesus," he cried, "don't you know there're *Injuns* out on the warpath?"

"Good for them," grumped Moore.

"Hell," said Champlain, "Injuns're about the only ones we ain't had trouble from."

Just then there was the sound of shots. All three turned and stared northward. Christ, thought Weasel, has Tompkins gone nuts again?

But he hadn't. This time the shots came from beyond the post. The guards atop the far ramparts, northeast corner, were waving, pointing, and shouting, "Someone's 'tackin' the Injun village!"

Conway, Cohen, and Lieutenant Smaldoon came crashing out of the orderly room. The guard house emptied out. The guard supernumeraries—those not slated for the next shift, as well as the customary extra guards—sprinted for the stables. But it was Mr. Allison who was the first to emerge, mounted on a horse, fired up for battle.

Before he ran down Moore and Champlain, the two privates had leaped onto their mounts and then, joined by Weasel, with Allison in the lead, the four had charged as one for the front gate. None had rifles, but all had their sidearms. If rifles were called for, the rest would bring them.

Captain Conway saw them racing and smiled briefly. Damn, they were eager to fight. "Who's that with Allison?"

Cohen squinted. "Moore, Champlain . . . and Weasel."

"Smaldoon! Form up that guard, take rifles, get the hell out there and back 'em up!" Conway shouted.

"Sir!" replied Smaldoon, already running toward the stables, shouting for a horse to be brought. And then Conway, as an afterthought, began charging the stables himself.

The front gate swung open so that Allison and his men didn't have to rein their horses in, just lean them into the sharp turn. Then they were beyond the gate, avoiding the telegraph poles and streaking for the village some quarter-mile distant.

Gillies let the other three string out in front of him, dropping the reins and checking the loads in his Scoffs. He always checked his rounds beforehand; a man didn't grow up careless in the slums, only short.

The tipis were getting bigger now, a rough semicircle open to the southeast, their backs to the prevailing winds. The tipis were canted just slightly back, if at all, and had three-pole supports—the village was primarily Cheyenne.

The soldiers guessed, from the positions of the Cheyenne within the village, that the attackers had never actually entered the village, but had fired from a distant draw. Halfway to the draw, lying awkwardly in the grass, were two bodies—Cheyenne, judging by the look of their clothing.

Allison swung around the outside of the village and bore down on the draw, pulling his guns and lying down alongside the neck of his horse. The rest imitated him.

Gunfire met them early, passing harmlessly wide and high, but by the time they gained the draw, the attackers had lit out. They went after them.

The draw ran on for a short distance, but then became clogged with brush and cottonwood, so they rode up out of it. That was when they spotted their prey, four men a couple of hundred yards ahead, raising dust for town.

Gillies was wondering if his horse, already run so far that day, was up to the chase. He hoped so because *he* sure was. And for once his size was a blessing.

The four men ahead had glanced back. They'd seen that they weren't being gained on noticeably, but were sure being chased. They threw shots back toward their pursuers, as much to warn as to actually hit anyone.

Allison and his men held their fire, concentrating on staying low and urging their horses on. Poor Moore, though, must have hung too low. One of the wild shots, which might have slid by or just nicked his waist, had he been upright, caught the bullet-headed private in the shoulder and carried him out of his saddle.

But his horse hardly slowed, and Gillies, figuring that

Moore couldn't have taken a square hit, ignored the fallen man and pulled up alongside Moore's horse. Holstering his guns, he leaped from his horse onto the other. Now the jockey-sized private had a comparatively fresh horse under him. He leaned into it and started kicking its flanks.

Gillies overtook and passed Champlain and Allison. His guns were back out, one hand also fingering the reins lightly.

He closed the distance.

Then he rose slightly in the stirrups. Fortunately, Moore hadn't had time to adjust them for his longer legs. He took galloping shocks in his legs, thereby steadying himself, and took aim and fired.

One of the pursued men had twisted around for a look-see, and just as he showed surprise at finding Gillies so close, he took the bullet in his gut.

Gillies' horse had to leap over the fallen man, losing a stride or two on the other three, but he soon made it up. He rose in his stirrups for another shot, but before he could trigger it, the three men had drawn up their horses and leaped to the ground. They figured they'd have a better chance with their fellow white man's mercy, maybe even understanding, than with soulless lead slugs. "Hey, we're *white*!" they shouted, and started to throw their guns down.

Not fast enough, though. Champlain, thundering up, had his gun misfire, but Gillies' didn't, and another man crumpled.

"Hold your fire, Weasel!" shouted Allison, having seen the men they were chasing drop their guns.

Gillies didn't manage to hold his fire, but he did tilt his gun up at the last second, sending the shot high.

Allison wondered why nobody fell down. Then he realized that Gillies had sent his shot wide. A little killer, he thought, but at least he'd followed orders.

Champlain was shaking his gun, cursing. Finally it went off, shooting a hole in a low cloud. "*Now* it works!" he exclaimed angrily.

"Gotta check 'em, Bu," said Gillies.

"I was *ridin'*. You checked yers?"

"Yep. An' I was ridin' too." It wasn't that Gillies wanted to demean Champlain's fighting expertise. Rather, he thought his life might someday depend on Champlain's gun going off properly.

"I'll *bet* you checked," sneered Buford, but he made a

112

mental note to check his own weapons in the future.

One of the captured men finally found his voice. "Jesus! What the hell you sojers shootin' *us* fer? Them's *Injuns* we shot, they warn't *white*. Them bastards scalped a buddy of mine, right in the middle of town. Whyn't you bastid blue-legs do somethin' about *that*, 'stead o' shootin' *us?*"

Allison stared coldly down at them.

"Can I kill 'em, Lieutenant?" begged Champlain.

Allison smiled thinly.

"An' the Injuns busted off the reservation," the man went on, ignoring Champlain. "Effin' war party, ever'body knows thet!"

"Not around here, they didn't," said Allison mildly.

The two men spent some time grousing, cursing, looking around angrily. Finally, "So? Whaddaya gonna do with us?" one asked.

"I figure we'll let you scoop your buddies up, unless you want to dig a hole for them here, and then—"

Captain Warner Conway, Lieutenant Smaldoon, and ten soldiers rode up just then, anxious to fight and consequently somewhat disappointed. "This is it, Mr. Allison?" asked Conway. "Just these two?"

"All that's left, sir. Apparently there were only four." He wiped his brow with a forearm. "Can't figure out, sir, why these dumbbells decided to go hunting Mr. Lo here, right on our front doorstep."

"It was a lesson," snarled one of the two men, "to get you off yer ass and *doin'* somethin'." Now his face fell as he realized just how successful they'd been.

The officers conferred, and it was decided that Mr. Allison and five men from the backup troop would take the two live men and their two dead companions into town and turn them over to the law. The size of the escort was intended to discourage any temper tantrums by the towns folk.

Captain Conway, Mr. Smaldoon, and the rest of the men then rode back to Outpost Number Nine, picking up the wounded Moore on the way.

Gillies and Champlain flanked Moore on the return.

"Lucky bastard," muttered Gillies, and Moore stared at him, fighting off pain and nausea. "This means you ain't gonna hafta go out an' work yer butt off like the rest of us."

Moore nodded, smiling grimly, not all that grateful.

seventeen ══════════════════

Quite a number of Indian settlements, large and small, were scattered over the High Plains, many within easy reach of Outpost Number Nine and Easy. They were, for the most part, Cheyenne and Sioux. Their inhabitants knew, or had heard of, the reservations where the Americans planned to relocate them, and they didn't want to go. They thought that if they remained peaceable and kept an extremely low profile, they might get to live outside those American "prisons." Indeed, it seemed as if the Americans were planning a "surround" of the red man, similar to the technique with which the Indian hunted buffalo: encircle and then tighten the circle.

Not surprisingly, many of those scattered villages were occupied by passive elements from the two tribes: the elderly, the women, and the very young. Not many warriors.

Such was the small village of Many Sons. The many sons to whom he owed his name had long since departed, gone to fight, to die, to flee northward. Many Sons was old and tired. He had killed Americans in his day, and many Crow, many Cree, many Assiniboine, many dead. Now he looked for peace, for time to smoke, for space to crawl upon the many wives he still possessed. He'd recently fathered two more children, and unless he'd lost track, he had several small grandchildren scattered about the village.

The sun had not been up too long. They had all eaten, a poor meal but freely earned, and now the children played their games in the dirt. And the women, many of them old, washed clothes in the nearby creek, bathed themselves, and brought water back.

114

They wash too much, thought Many Sons, disparaging the recently acquired American custom. He liked the way they used to smell. He himself washed rarely.

He heard the shots and frowned.

The women and children came running from the creek.

And then the riders were upon them, their guns speaking deadly thunder.

Many Sons could not remember where he'd left his gun, an old Springfield, a relic, a single-shot muzzle-loader. It was a good gun, good enough to down the buffalo. But it would not have been enough to stem this American tide . . . even if he'd had a chance to use it.

The rider came swiftly from the east toward Outpost Number Nine raising a small cloud of dust in his wake. Tompkins, again stationed atop the lookout tower, stared at the distant, oncoming rider but didn't make a move or a sound. Hell, the entire Sioux Nation could be descending on Easy and he wouldn't have uttered a peep. To hell with all those bastards, treating him like they did. Serve them right if Mr. Lo *did* wipe them out.

"Sure rides like an Injun, don't he?" murmured Sergeant of the Guard Breckenridge at his shoulder.

Tompkins barely managed not to jump straight up in the air. He made a grunting sound.

"Must've heard you was here, Private. Comin' to get you. You're a famous Injun fighter."

Tompkins made another noise.

"Figured you'd have your gun heated up real good by now. Turned over a new leaf or somethin'?"

Tompkins had about the sharpest eyes on the post, but he also had an easily fevered imagination.

"All right, Tompkins, he's close enough now. Who the hell is it?"

"One of Windy's scouts. Turpentine or somethin'."

Close, thought Breckenridge. Turning Wind was the man's name. Delaware. Lived with the nearby Cheyenne, but owed no allegiance to any tribe. Probably figured he was white by now.

The gate opened and Turning Wind rode in, heading straight for the orderly room.

Captain Conway was standing by Sergeant Cohen's desk,

going over the morning report with the sergeant—Moore laid up with his wound; two other men sick with what might be scurvy, damn fools, wasn't necessary, their fault, not Dutch's; and a fourth man, after a night in town, with the runs, another fool—when Turning Wind entered.

The scout's face, like any Indian's, gave nothing away. Conway glanced at him and saw nothing to cause alarm.

"What's up, Wind?" asked Sergeant Cohen, damned if he was going to run down the complete names of these fellows every time.

"East. Cheyenne. Many Sons."

Conway smiled. "*That* old goat. Heard he had some more kids. How is he?"

"Dead." Suddenly the scout had their undivided attention. "All dead."

"Who . . . ?" Conway began.

"White men. Ten, fifteen riders, maybe more."

"The women?" wondered Conway. "Children?"

"Dead."

"Lid's blowin' off, Captain," said Cohen.

"Damn!" groaned Conway. "It's been building up. Mr. Lo doesn't know anything about farming, about ranching, about grazing rights. A rancher wakes up one morning and there's a whole village squatting just over the next rise, camped by his water hole."

"They think it's their land too," said Turning Wind. "It used to be theirs."

Captain Conway stared at him, this strange scout he rarely encountered. "I know that," he said, annoyed. "Everybody knows that. But Washington says it's not their land. That's policy."

"The Indian doesn't understand that," Turning Wind said.

Conway, almost blinded by sudden anger, thought furiously: That's all I need now, a discussion of Indian policy and philosophy with one of Windy's scouts.

"They go back down south?" Conway asked, calming himself. "Head for some town, Rock Creek maybe?"

"No, north."

North? Conway racked his brains, then looked to Cohen and the scout for help.

"Red Lance," said Cohen.

"Oh, God."

116

"And he ain't no sissy," added Ben.

"Form a patrol, Sergeant. Allison. Breckenridge—"

"Breck's got guard, sir."

"Sergeant Olsen, then."

"In which case it'd better be Mr. Price, sir," said Sergeant Cohen. "I ain't certain, but I figure Mr. Price'd probably prefer being shot to being left behind and insulted."

First Platoon was Mr. Price's, and if Olsen and elements of the First were going out, then Price should probably go with them. He had in the past, many times. It was a fact, though, that on most if not all of those occasions, Matt Kincaid was along to keep Price out of trouble. But Price on his own? . . .

"Trust Olsen, sir," said Ben Cohen. "He'll take care of him."

"Okay, get 'em mounted, Sergeant. It's time Mr. Price found out what it's all about."

"What *what* is all about?" asked Price, coming through the door looking extremely dapper. If nothing else, his wife, Polly, had shaped up his appearance.

"I know how you've been aching for action, Mr. Price," said Captain Conway.

Price stopped dead, staring at him, not sure he was hearing right.

Ben Cohen may have thought that Red Lance wasn't a sissy, but Ben was going from considerably distant history. What he didn't know was that in Red Lance's last battle he'd had an arm, his right, nearly severed, had cut the rest off himself, had escaped scalping, and had recovered. The missing arm had become a kind of badge of honor, a symbol of mourning, worth all the fingers in the entire Crow Nation, with whom he was not friendly. But it also ended his warring days. And it would have ended a lot more—he couldn't even fill his own pipe—had he not been surrounded by a people still eager to do his bidding and follow his leadership.

And his leadership had been peaceful. So peaceful, in fact, that many young braves from his village had politely excused themselves and gone abroad in search of excitement.

Those braves, nominally Cheyenne, had then drifted into a slightly different sphere of influence: Sioux, a band under Silver Fox that had recently begun to explore peaceful village living, and was not too happy with the experience. The Sioux

117

were now committed to peace and a kind of village-oriented agrarian reform, but damn, they sure weren't happy. There was unrest from the leadership all the way down, which created a climate that the expatriate Cheyenne not only found congenial, but to which they could add their own discontent. It seemed only a matter of days, if not hours, before the entire village took up arms and went on a rampage.

This Sioux village of Silver Fox was some distance north of that of Red Lance, but not totally out of reach. Red Lance knew the Sioux were camped within a few hours' ride, and that his own braves had joined them, but he didn't want to have anything to do with them. He distrusted Silver Fox. The man would meet the Americans' treachery with his own, match lie for lie. It was not good.

Red Lance was watching a comely woman pack a pipe for him while another woman prepared some ground for him to sit upon, when the riders were suddenly among them.

Silver Fox was restless, unable to stand still, pacing about the encampment, ready to arm himself, mount up, and lead his warriors back out on the trail to glory. He was no longer young, but he was not ready to pass his days tilling soil or milking cows. That was, at best, women's work and dishonorable. He understood that at one time, beyond memory of the eldest, his people had dwelt far to the east and had lived in one place, from the soil and land about them. But that was before the Sioux became the great nation of the Plains.

He gripped his rifle, a carbine repeater. It felt good. It was the white man's weapon and it felt good. Silver Fox's smile was cruel. Yes, he would follow the white man's way, with the white man's weapon, behave as the white man had taught them.

Kill. Kill from ambush, kill from cover, kill with deceit. It was the white man's way. The American way.

Buffalo Grass, one of the Cheyenne expatriates, watched Silver Fox closely. The great chief would soon know no restraint. Buffalo Grass wondered about his sisters, whether they were safe and what they were doing. If Buffalo Grass wanted to see his people again, perhaps for the last time, it had to be now.

He quietly selected a fine pony and sprang astride. He rode

it at a walk from the cluster of tipis. No one paid any attention.

Once clear of the village, he kicked his pony into a run, smiling as he felt the wind rush against his face and curl around his body....

A bright flash of light caught his eye. He looked ahead into the distance.

Riders. The sun had reflected from shiny metal. He slowed, steadying his vision.

Americans. Armed. Riding hard toward him. Many Americans.

Buffalo Grass ducked his horse down into a draw, twisted it around, and rode back the way he'd come. But not quite the same way. He stayed off the high ground as much as he could, and when he couldn't avoid it, he bent low on his horse, sometimes hanging over the side out of sight, and walked him to the next dip. If the Americans saw anything, they'd see just a horse.

Buffalo Grass raced into the Sioux camp and alit at the feet of Silver Fox. "Americans come. With guns. I fear they come to attack."

Silver Fox smiled. "We will meet them. We will let them come and deliver their scalps to us." It was a fine turn of events.

"There are many, Silver Fox, as many warriors as we have, and the guns they carry, they are the long ones, the ones that can kill from beyond the mountain."

It was an exaggeration, but the new Sharps rifles, the ones with the .50-caliber slug powered by seventy grains of black powder, could tear a hole in a buffalo from ranges almost as far as a man could accurately see.

Silver Fox looked about. There was no good cover. The Americans could stay in the distance and pick them off, much the way they did when they killed the buffalo.

Just then the band of whites came into view some six to seven hundred yards distant.

Let us draw them close, thought Silver Fox. He told his braves to act normally, move slowly, but find their weapons and get ready.

The whites weren't having any of that, though. They realized that the Sioux must have seen them, that there was no chance for a surprise attack, and they weren't about to ride into range of the Indian carbines. And with their buffalo guns, they didn't have to. There'd be plenty of time later to saunter in and pick up scalps.

The whites hit the ground well beyond effective carbine and Springfield range, took up sitting or prone positions, and started laying a blanket of fire down on the village.

The Sioux stayed behind what little cover they could find. For the most part they escaped injury, but their horses took off and tipis began to sag and collapse at random as .50-caliber slugs splintered the support poles. The Sioux saw death drawing near.

Thus was the error of violent ways brought crushingly home to Silver Fox. Even had his namesake, the wily fox, been present, he would have been hard-pressed to find a way out.

But there was still a chance. Stay hidden, be patient; the Americans would have to come closer.

And the white men did begin to advance. But at closer range their shots were more accurate. Among them were men who could shoot a fly off a buffalo's rump at three hundred yards.

Silver Fox, humiliated, ground his face into the soil. But that, he vowed, would be his last act of self-effacement. He had decided to rise and charge. Better to die a man than a prairie dog.

But when he did rise, hearing the continuing thunder of guns and expecting to be met by a hail of bullets, he found himself miraculously unscathed. The Great Spirit was with him. He started forward.

But when he looked to the distance, to the Americans, he saw the reason for his escape. The Americans were still firing their guns, but in the opposite direction. Perhaps some Sioux or Cheyenne war party had come up behind them.

Then he saw the Americans leaping to their feet, pointing their guns down or discarding them. And then, beyond them, other men rose and approached, rifles at the ready. Men in blue. Soldiers.

Lieutenant Price, Sergeant Olsen, and the squad-sized patrol had raced for Red Lance's camp, led by Turning Wind. After a while they came across the tracks of the white raiders. But while the patrol had been riding northeast, the raiders' tracks ran north.

"Which way is the village, scout?" asked Price.

Turning Wind pointed northeast.

"Then they're going the wrong way, probably lost. Come on, maybe we can beat them to the village."

But no one charged off. Price, after all, wasn't really in charge of the patrol, unless he insisted.

"Anyone else you know about around here, Turning Wind?" asked Sergeant Olsen, a sober, steady Swede and, in his own way, as good as any of Easy's other NCOs.

Turning Wind shook his head slowly.

"You ain't sure, though."

Turning Wind shook his head even more slowly.

"Mr. Price," said Olsen, "maybe they're lost and maybe they ain't. Might be a good idea if you took the scout and three of the men and headed on into the village. I'll follow the tracks. Don't worry, I been followin' tracks since I was knee-high to a grasshopper. That way, sir, if they are lost, or tryin' to circle around, and they end up attackin' anyway, we'll get 'em in a crossfire. . . ."

Price was frowning, trying to simply keep track of Olsen's reasoning. "Errr, good thinking, Sergeant. We'll do that." He smiled wanly. "Seems simple enough."

And Lieutenant Price, the scout, and three privates rode off toward the village.

Olsen watched them go, sorry to lose manpower but seeing no choice. Price had had his mind set on Red Lance's village, and Olsen wasn't up to an argument. But the sergeant did guess that the raiders had something other than Red Lance's Cheyenne in mind. They seemed to know where they were going— their tracks told Olsen they'd been riding hard without hesitation—and Olsen just wished he knew what and where it was.

He led his men, six including Corporal Milier and men from First Platoon's second and third squads, off along the trail left by the raiders.

It wasn't too long before they heard the distant firing, a couple of hours at most.

And then they came within sight of the one-sided battle. Olsen saw that the raiders were hammering the village from beyond the range of the Indians' guns. The trouble was that the army's guns weren't any better than the Indians'. They were going to have to get a lot closer before their own trap-door Springfields could be effective.

They crawled forward, cursing mildly, through the high, sometimes rapier-sharp grass.

At length they'd crawled to within range of the raiders, whereupon they started laying down fire.

The raiders reacted swiftly, except for the two that were hit by the first army volley. They twisted around, took better cover, and returned the fire. They couldn't see who their attackers were—probably thought some damn hostiles had snuck up behind them—and weren't too happy or comfortable, but they weren't really worried. No hostile was going to get any closer than their buffalo guns allowed. . . .

Then they saw more riders approaching in the deeper distance. The army, for crying out loud!

Then they saw the army joining those who'd been firing at them, and that gave them even more to think about.

Finding the Cheyenne village peaceful, its headman, Red Lance, owning just one arm and about to settle down on a blanket with a pipe, Lieutenant Price reacted the same way Olsen had and rode right on back out of the village. He was not far behind Olsen—close enough, in fact, to hear Olsen and his detachment fire their first rounds at the bushwhackers shooting at Silver Fox's village.

As it happened, the visibility of Price and his men, as they rode into the fray, helped bring the battle to an end, as the raiders became aware that they were not being fired upon by Indians, but rather by the U.S. Army, which was an entirely different kettle of fish. Immediately the raiders started yelling for a ceasefire.

Price was yelling too, from a rather undignified position on the ground. He was also trying to remove himself from under the somewhat overweight, limp body of one Private Kemperer, lying unconscious athwart him. Kemperer had belatedly recognized the deep boom of the raiders' buffalo guns, and had instantly dragged Price from his saddle with the properly soldierly notion of protecting his superior officer. Unfortunately, Kemperer had managed to get himself accidentally whacked on the head by Price's mount's rear hoof, which, luckily, didn't kill him, but certainly left him in a state of blissful slumber atop Mr. Price.

Within a few moments, however, Kemperer had regained

122

consciousness and Price had recovered some of his dignity.

Three of the raiders had been killed in the fray, and they were wrapped in tarps and thrown across the saddles of their own horses. The living members of the party were also in their own saddles, trussed up, their horses roped together. They would be escorted in this fashion back to Easy Company's guardhouse, where they would remain until the civilian law could be summoned to take them off the army's hands. How they would fare in the white man's court was anybody's guess.

"But they won't be seein' much more action for a long time, I reckon," said Sergeant Olsen to Silver Fox.

The Sioux chief eyed Olsen. The Swede did not cut a prepossessing figure, but he'd certainly pulled the Sioux' fat out of the fire. "You are good," said Silver Fox. "Some Americans bad, some good. You are good."

Olsen showed Silver Fox a smile and a reasonable facsimile of a peace sign. And then the patrol moved out, herding its prisoners along, with Mr. Price casting suspicious sidelong glances toward Private Kemperer.

For his own part, Silver Fox put his plans for violence and insurrection on the shelf . . . for the time being, anyway.

eighteen _____

Lieutenant Matt Kincaid and his men rode west across Montana in pursuit of the Crow. The trail led them along the Musselshell toward that river's headwaters, high in the Rockies. They split the distance between Fort Howe to the north and Bozeman to the south, as they left the Musselshell to follow the hard-driving Crow up Flathead Creek.

Radersburgh was dead ahead, over on the far side of the Missouri, which, in this early stage of its life, was flowing from south to north before it turned east to cross Montana. It was one hell of a long river once you got to know it; a person could cross the Missouri at the northeast corner of Kansas, ride northwest for some fifteen hundred miles, and then have to cross the Missouri all over again. But the Crow band rode north of Radersburgh and continued west.

Where the hell were they going? Matt wondered. They and their quarry had passed plenty of Indian sign, some Blackfoot, some Flathead, but the Crow had apparently shown no interest, as if they had a specific destination in mind.

The Easy Company patrol kept climbing. They were well into the Rockies now, riding higher and higher through gold and silver country. The Continental Divide wasn't too far ahead.

They reached it late the third day. The Crow trail that Windy had kept his hooks into turned south at that point, as if to follow the high ground. Matt decided to stop for the night in the vicinity of Frederickson.

It was a mining town primarily, but there were also ranches

in the vicinity, lodged in the high valleys, so it wasn't just a one-business town. In fact, it figured to be a hell of a lot more than that.

A couple of well-dressed men, bankers probably, took the time to bend an elbow and chat with Matt and Sergeant Chubb in one of the local saloons.

"Right nearby, no more'n five miles away's the proposed route of the Northern Pacific. It'll head north into Washington and all the way to the Pacific. And going the other way, it'll hook us up with Bozeman and points east. Anyone coming from Chicago, say, to the Northwest is going to have to come right by here. Figure we'll have us a spur off the main line right into town. So! How's *that* sound?"

"Real fine," said Matt. "When's it due?"

"I understand they're into Montana already, headin' our way."

"Don't think so," said Sergeant Chubb. "I been east of Montana a ways and I ain't seen them."

"Well, it's supposed to be finished all the way to the Coast by '83. Naturally, they're layin' it down from the west too. In fact, just north of here, at Gold Creek, which is just east of New Chicago, that's where the lines are supposed to join up. Guess we'll be havin' a big celebration along about then."

"Guess so," agreed Matt.

"What are you boys doing out this way?"

"Chasing Indians," said Matt. "Have you seen any?"

"I should hope not. You mean hostiles, don't you? No, thank the Lord, I haven't. But then, the Nez Perce are north of here and I've heard something's going on with them..."

"Injuns," growled the other banker. "Should have said we'd be celebrating the Northern Pacific come '83, *Injuns permitting*. I've got me some Injun stories that'll curl your hair, if you boys would like to hear..."

The patrol moved out at the crack of dawn the next day. They'd grained their horses in Frederickson and the mounts were raring to go. They traveled swiftly southwest, heading for Idaho.

"Where the hell are they headed, Windy?" asked Matt.

Windy didn't know and just spat and shook his head.

They came across a wagon and four dead men. The men had been scalped and their wagon emptied of foodstuffs and ammunition.

"Ain't too far ahead, Matt, and they really done crossed the divide."

Matt looked at Windy. It was his impression that they were right on top of the Divide, but Windy explained that it wasn't the *Continental* Divide he was talking about.

"Back at the settlement, in killin' them whites, you might've said they was intolerably provoked. Not this time, though. They've gone bad, out for blood, red, white, or blue, don't matter nohow. That's the divide I mean."

Matt nodded grimly.

They pressed on rapidly. They were circling a stand of pine and brush when Windy suddenly drew his horse up, stared at the ground, and then uphill toward the stand of growth. And then he was leaving the saddle, a shout barely out of his mouth, when they suddenly took fire from the trees. Felson pitched from his saddle, dead before he hit the ground.

The patrol flew from their mounts. Fortunately for them, the terrain was rocky enough for them to find cover.

They first looked to where Felson lay exposed, searching for some sign of life. But he lay so still he might have been a rock himself. They turned their attention back to the stand of pine. Kincaid signaled Chubb and Plowright to move in for a conference.

Neither man looked happy about crawling through rocks and gunfire to parley, but they did.

"Trail runs down a ways and turns up over that rise, doesn't it, Windy?"

"Looks that way to me," said the scout, cradling his Winchester. "Guess we caught 'em, didn't we?"

Matt scowled at him. "Plowright, take your squad, work your way down toward the bend, to where you can command the trail up over the rise. They may try to come out that way. In fact they probably will; going straight back over the top, they'd expose themselves. So you just lay in there and cover the trail. Chubb, we'll hang in here, and lay down some fire to cover Plowright while he gets his men in place. Then, when I give the signal, we'll start to move forward. We'll have good cover if we take it slow. Now, if it works, it'll squeeze them out your end, Plowright, so you make sure you and your men have good and steady shooting positions before you make your moves forward. Don't want you running full-tilt just when they're showing themselves. You got that?"

"Got it, sir!" cried Plowright with unexpected zest. "They've got white women with them, don't they, sir?"

Matt frowned. "I *hope* they've still got them." He was beginning to understand Plowright's fervor. The son of a bitch figured he was defending all of white womanhood. Considering Clara Plowright, it was ridiculous. Matt almost changed his mind and replaced Plowright with Chubb, but he didn't, even though Chubb would have been the better choice from the start.

It could have been that Matt was deliberately, if unconsciously, putting Plowright's life at risk, but that was a question that would never have an answer. And *somebody* had to cover that left flank.

In any event, it was moot because Plowright, inspired by his holy cause, had already gone scurrying off to round up his squad.

"We're *what*?" Matt heard someone exclaim in the direction Plowright had taken. Sounded like Kazmaier.

Matt sent Chubb off to organize his men. Then, after a decent pause, he poked his head up cautiously and brought his rifle around to bear on the stand of pine.

The scrub pine was pretty short. If a man stood up, his head might clear the tops. Matt didn't see any heads. He *did* think he saw movement and a glint of sun on steel, and he fired. And he thought he'd scored a hit, but he wasn't sure. Where a white man might be expected to yowl in pain, Mr. Lo often didn't make a peep. Chubb and his men picked up the fire, and Plowright and his detail went crawling.

Barrett/Bloody Arm/Medicine Calf crouched in the scrub pine, concealed additionally by small boulders. He hadn't wanted to stand and make a fight, but Kincaid—he'd recognized Matt—had been sticking to their trail like a bloodhound and making up too much ground. It was time to bring *that* to a sudden halt.

They'd pulled off the trail four hours earlier and waited patiently. But they'd been careless to leave that sign where Windy could spot it. He'd underestimated Windy.

He supposed he could have killed Kincaid with that first shot, but he'd chosen Felson instead. He'd never cared for Felson.

They'd all left their horses before he'd had a chance to see who else was along. But now he didn't have time. He'd planned

127

to decimate the patrol with that first volley, but the plan had gone awry; the Crow just weren't quite eager enough to shoot from cover and their delay might prove fatal. It would certainly prove fatal unless he could bring big medicine to bear and figure out how to score tellingly and get away.

He outnumbered Matt, but he didn't delude himself into thinking his Crow could outfight Matt and the men from Easy, man to man. Matt's men were almost all fighters, and blooded too often to go down easily, if at all. Barrett decided he was going to have to probe for a weak spot and exploit it.

What would the great Crow war chief, the mulatto Jim Beckwith, have done? Probably jumped up and yelled, "Hey, don't shoot, I'm white, we're Crow, we're friends!" There were drawbacks to following certain visions. And there weren't any that were perfect, Barrett was finding that out.

Barrett had his men strung out strategically. He'd talked them out of charging and committing suicide, but apparently had not talked them into laying down a volley worthy of the name. Well, hell, win some, lose some. He could afford to be philosophical; they were still in a good, commanding position. Now all he had to do was wait for a winning gambit to present itself.

He hunkered down on his heels as a round whined overhead. It might be a long wait. Maybe they should shoot the army horses, standing back a ways. But he couldn't bring himself to order such carnage. Not yet, anyway.

He glanced off at an angle, between two boulders, having only that one narrow line of sight to the army line.

Movement. He saw movement. He scrunched around and concentrated on the spot.

There it was again, one man, then another, leaping from behind one rock to behind another. And the one leading them, the first in line, he thought he recognized a familiar bulk, a familiar, foolish shape—bends his head and thinks he's crouched.

Blowhard! Blowhard Plowright. Damn, the Great Spirit was moving in very friendly ways to put *that* asshole up against him.

Where was he heading? For the flank, for the trail over the rise? Maybe so, but if Barrett knew Matt Kincaid, Blowhard hadn't been entrusted with any flanking action; Kincaid had to know better than that.

They were probably just getting into position to cover the trail—and cover their escape, dammit!—ready to move forward in a line with the rest.

Barrett's eyes narrowed. He had the two young women and the boy over on the right flank, with Buffalo Hump keeping an eye on them.

The women hadn't been any trouble. One of them, Alice (not the prettiest, Lame Dog had gotten that one), had been real nice, had made his nights very pleasant once she'd gotten used to it, had started cuddling up real sweet. And to the boy it was almost a game. He'd make a fine warrior someday. Hell, the kid didn't have any folks left, maybe Barrett would adopt him. Or Lame Dog might, if they could figure out which girl he was brother to.

But all that would happen only if they got out of this fix, he reminded himself. Blowhard. He concentrated on remembering what he knew of the sergeant, summoning forth all the man's weaknesses. . . .

He'd use one of the girls. He didn't like risking them, but he had to. They might get hurt, but if he knew Plowright . . .

Ernie Plowright had his men in position, a little forward of where they were supposed to be, but not so far as to get Kincaid excited. Plowright just wanted to get as close as he could to those kidnapping, raping red bastards.

He heard the firing continue down to his right. And he too threw some random shots toward the stand of pine.

Then the firing from the pines diminished, died down, and stopped. Plowright braced himself, figuring the Indians were fixing to charge.

But then . . .

Up the trail, near the top of the rise, an Indian came out of the pines, holding one of the white women in front of him, a knife at her throat.

Plowright's vocal chords got all tangled up and he nearly strangled himself but he managed to croak, "Hold your fire, hold your goddamn fire, goddammit! That's a *white* woman."

As he and his men watched, waiting, grinding their teeth, some twenty to thirty Crow raced from the pines and fled over the rise.

Heading for their horses, Plowright decided.

Finally, all had vanished over the crest except for the brave holding the white female hostage. And those last two were about to follow, when the girl broke free and ran toward Plowright's men, yelping. But the brave, Lame Dog it was, overtook her in a flash, seized her, and dragged her back up the hill, all the time keeping the yelping girl between himself and the soldiers.

Matt wondered what was going on. He'd heard someone yelling. Sounded like Plowright. But that had been a while ago. Nothing since.

But that was mainly because Plowright had been shocked, transfixed. But now he shook free of the spell. The graphic drama mounted right before his horrified eyes had been too much. Rape! Mutilation! It was too much for his white manliness to take. And as soon as Lame Dog and the white girl had dropped from sight, he leaped to his feet, brandishing his rifle, waving his men forward.

"C'mon! They're mountin' up, we can catch 'em before they can get away!"

Matt's eyes popped as he saw Plowright and his squad leap to their feet and dash up the trail.

"What the hell . . . *Plowright*!" roared Matt.

Then, cursing, he leaped to his feet, only to be driven back down by fire from the pines.

"Bloody Plowright," groaned Matt. "Bloody, effin' Plowright." He knew he should have sent Chubb over there.

Plowright heard the firing from the pines, but it didn't register because they weren't firing at him. He scrambled forward in mad haste.

Nearing the crest, he saw the distant torsos, and then heads, of retreating Crow. He nearly went mad, redoubling his efforts. He'd have been better advised to note that the retreating Crow were comparatively few in numbers.

The adrenaline pumped him up over the crest of the rise at high speed, his men close behind, eager for the kill.

Once they'd topped the rise and were getting ready to throw lead after the retreating Crow, the members of Barrett's band who *hadn't* fled, who were concealed on the flanks, opened fire on Plowright and his men.

Plowright and his men dropped like stones.

The Crow closed in from the flanks. And the Crow that had been left behind to pin down Matt and the rest came hustling over the ridge. Coups were lying about, waiting to be counted.

But Matt and Sergeant Chubb had known what was going to happen to Plowright and his men before it happened. It was an old Indian trick, suckering the enemy into a trap, and almost everyone knew about it and thereby neutralized the gambit. The lure must have been powerful to get Plowright charging blindly into it. Matt, knowing there were white women available for display, had a pretty good idea what the lure was.

In any event, as soon as the firing from the pines abated, which happened before the Crow opened up on Plowright (it was a carefully timed maneuver), Matt knew the rear guard was pulling out. And so did Chubb.

The two men leaped to their feet and started running like hell for the trail and then up it. The men followed. Stretch, in fact, all six feet, seven inches of him, began to overtake them.

Matt knew that lives and scalps hung in the balance. Fortunately he and Chubb, whose bony, slim silhouette belied his name, were in good condition and moved like frightened deer.

They topped the rise to find scalps being taken. Matt's guns started thundering, his close-work pistols. Chubb dropped his rifle too, and also went to work with his handguns. Then the rest of the soldiers arrived, blasting.

Ten Crow went down, right on top of their army victims. The rest scattered, leaped astride horses on the run, and joined the rest of the Crow, farther on down the hill. Then the entire band took off, except for one man who remained at the bottom of the hill. He was within rifle range, a brave mounted on an army horse, but he had one of the white women sitting behind him. A bullet might hit her as easily as the brave. The hostile's voice carried up to Matt, faintly but clearly.

"Bloody Arm salutes you, Kincaid, you are a brave warrior. But you are not strong enough. The coups you took, we also took. We are strong still, and you are weak, and our medicine is strong. I, Medicine Calf, now lead my people to the peaceful valley where we will live and fight no more. Do not follow. Medicine Calf, war chief of the Absaroka, is too strong." Then the warrior turned his horse away and rode after the Crow.

Matt couldn't recognize him, but he knew damned well he'd heard the madman, Barrett. But what the hell was all that "Bloody Arm" crap? And "Medicine Calf"?

"Sir," shouted Malone, "let's go after them."

Matt looked around. Chubb, his face long as he poked

through the bodies, gave Malone a look of censure. Matt said, "We took some of him, but he took too goddamn much of us. We're going to have to pass him on to someone else. Now come on, let's see what we've got here."

Besides the ten dead Crow, there were seven dead soldiers, damn near all of Plowright's squad. Plowright, though, was still alive, lying beneath a private who'd been finished off with a knife and then scalped. Two other men had escaped with bad, but not critical, wounds.

Plowright's wounds, though, *were* critical, if not immediately fatal. Two of them were flesh wounds, in his upper torso, and were quickly patched. The third wound, however—well, that might also, with callous indifference, have been called a flesh wound—his genitals had been shot away.

The bleeding was heavy from that wound, and Matt, seeing it, was tempted to let him bleed to death.

Plowright, barely conscious, seemed to divine his thoughts. "It is," he said weakly, "most certainly...God's will... Lieutenant."

The blood flow was stanched as much as possible. Then a travois was constructed in which, after it was attached to a horse, Plowright was gently laid. The two other wounded men proved able to ride unaided. And seeing that they were going to have to return to Outpost Number Nine, Matt decided they'd take their dead with them, hoping they'd reach the post before the corpses started stinking too badly.

They let the Crow lie where they fell, for their flesh to decay and their bones to be picked clean by buzzards and coyotes. It could be that the Crow would return sometime later, to gather the bones and give them a decent burial.

Windy led them east some fifty miles, over mountain passes and through high valleys, to Virginia City in Madison County, a city of nearly a thousand inhabitants, a city built on gold and silver.

A doctor looked at Plowright while Matt sent news of their defeat and imminent return to Captain Conway. He also shot off wires to various military posts in territories to the southwest, advising them of the Crow presence.

Later the doctor told Matt that Plowright was in bad shape. The medic had stitched up the femoral artery as best he could, but Plowright would need months of medical attention. However, he could be transported if it was done carefully.

Leaving the doctor, Matt told Sergeant Chubb, "Find a wagon. Then you, Windy, and the men take Plowright back to the post. Make sure he doesn't start bleeding again." Matt stared at the ground. "Poor bastard."

"He ain't so unhappy," muttered Windy.

Matt looked up and stared at Windy. He waited for more, but didn't get it.

"All right," he finally said, "I'm heading for Keogh. I've got to see someone there. Might even beat you back to Easy."

He grinned, mounted up, and rode off.

He had something like three hundred miles ahead of him, just to get to Keogh. After that . . .

Damn. He wished the effin' railroad tracks had already been laid.

nineteen _____

"Goddamn it all to hell," Sergeant Cohen swore on his way into Captain Conway's office.

Conway looked up. "What is it, Ben?"

"Aw, just bad news, sir. Bradshaw just took a wire from Lieutenant Kincaid. Seems he got ambushed somewheres up near Virginia City. Lost seven men. Eight, if you count Plowright."

Conway closed his eyes and leaned back wearily, then asked, "What about Plowright?"

"Bad hurt, sir. Don't say right out, but I figure he might've got his balls shot off."

Conway grimaced involuntarily. Neither he nor Cohen commented on it, but the irony of this turn of events was not lost on either of them. They were silent for a moment, then Cohen went on, "The men are comin' back with Chubb and Windy, but Lieutenant Kincaid's headed for Keogh, he don't say why."

Conway nodded; he had an idea why. Then he asked, "Tell me, Ben, just how many men have we got available at the moment?"

"Well, sir"—Cohen began to count off on his fingers—"we got Dutch and his crack-shot cooks, and ol' Skinflint in supply, with that corporal of his, and a couple of men cleanin' out the stables while there ain't too many horses on post. . . ." By this time he'd used up two hands' worth of fingers.

"And you and me and Corporal Bradshaw," Conway finished.

"Don't know as I'd include Bradshaw, sir, unless he can

134

hit someone with his telegraph key or stab 'em with a pencil."
He grinned. "But we got patrols guardin' about every Indian
settlement we can think of. Mr. Lo's never had it so goddamn
safe. Let's just hope *he* don't start to make no trouble."

Conway shook his head. "Wouldn't be a hell of a lot to be
said for either side. There's a story about Mr. Lincoln watching
a man wrestle a bear and—an eminently fair man, Mr. Lincoln—all he could bring himself to shout was, 'Go, man, Go,
bear.'"

"Be that as it may, sir," Cohen said, "I don't figure we'll
be getting much trouble from Mr. Lo in the real near future."

The Union Pacific rolled north out of Laramie, Wyoming, and
passed through the towns of Howell, Cooper's Lake, Lookout,
and Miser. Next along the line was Rock Creek. After that,
Wilcox and then Como. The train was carrying the month's
payroll for the various forts and outposts scattered over the
Laramie plains. It would be met by an armed guard at Como.
Before it got to Rock Creek, though, it came a cropper. Or the
payroll shipment did, anyway.

The train was rolling smoothly along, its view ahead clear
for some distance, until there appeared a blockage on the rails.

The engineer slowed the train as he peered down the line.
He made out the shapes of four, maybe five, steers lying dead,
two directly on the tracks, the other two or three lying nearby.
Rotten luck, thought the engineer, for the cows *and* the Union
Pacific.

He stopped the train a few feet short of the carcasses. He
yelled back that they had dead steers blocking the way, and
called for someone to come up and drag them clear.

The door of the first baggage car opened and five army
privates jumped out, guards for the army payroll shipment. An
officer also jumped out, intent on supervising the dragging.

The carcasses lay in a pretty tight group, practically piled
on top of one another. The soldiers were just about to take hold
of the topmost carcasses when six Indians materialized, rising
up from behind the cows. Six Indians with repeaters.

The guns roared repeatedly.

The five privates and the officer went down immediately.
The Indians ran to the baggage car, shooting the engineer and
his fireman on the way—neither fatally—and relieved the train
of the army payroll.

A seventh Indian appeared in the distance and rode toward the train, leading six Indian ponies.

The Indian whoops blended with cries of alarm from the passenger section of the train. Those passengers, hearing the bloodcurdling howls, feared for their scalps. Given their druthers, they'd prefer plain old white American train robbers.

And then the Indians were gone, much the richer.

The passengers slowly disembarked and came forward to see what had happened. Among them were several strong men. They tossed the bodies of the army men into the baggage car and cleared the tracks while others propped the wounded engineer up so he could get the damn train moving. One really anxious fellow volunteered to shovel the coal. And so the train did start rolling west again. But the guard detachment waiting two stops farther along at Como was going to have a long wait.

Corporal "Four Eyes" Bradshaw cautiously entered Captain Conway's office. The captain appeared to be asleep, reclining in the chair behind his desk. Bradshaw turned and started to leave.

"Yes, Corporal, what is it?" The voice was weary enough for its owner actually to have been asleep.

Mrs. Conway had been in a playful mood the night before, and although such exertions usually left her husband bright and cheerful throughout the morning, by afternoon he was beginning to run down a bit. He was approaching the age where he needed a full night's sleep to get him through the next day.

"Sergeant Cohen isn't here, sir."

"I know that. *He* got a full night's sleep."

"Sir?"

"And now he's probably running around the parade, doing his daily dozen laps."

"Sergeant *Cohen*? . . . Sir?"

Conway nodded sleepily, smiling, amused by his own wit. "Anything special you wanted him for, Corporal?"

"Just a message, sir."

"Well, you can tell me, can't you? I may not be as influential around here as Sergeant Cohen, but I am not without *some* importance." Conway's eyes were still closed. Bradshaw had the unpleasant feeling of addressing a sleepwalker, or a sleep-*talker*, anyway.

"Train robbery, sir. Near Rock Creek. Indians, sir."

136

"Indians," Conway mused, eyes sealed. "Fancy that, after all we're doing for them. They steal some jewelry or something?"

"Nossir."

"Anyone hurt?"

"Yessir. Two wounded and six dead. Six soldiers."

"Soldiers," Conway repeated softly. "What would they—" His eyes suddenly snapped open and he came erect in his chair, like a released catapult, scaring the shit out of Bradshaw. "The *payroll!*" he yelled. "The army payroll! Those bastards!" He seethed. *"Sergeant Cohen!"* he roared, and the roof practically lifted off the orderly room.

And Sergeant Cohen, almost choking on his pudding, jumped up and raced from the mess.

"Sergeant," said Conway to his panting first sergeant, "get a patrol together, a *combat* patrol. Those goddamned hostiles have robbed the payroll."

Sergeant Cohen, despite his breathlessness, was galvanized. "I can get Breckenridge in with his men," said Cohen, figuring it out aloud as he returned to his desk, "and I know where Miller is with *his* squad. Bradshaw!"

"Sarge?"

"Get those men here from the stables. Tell 'em to bring horses."

"Right, Sarge." Bradshaw ran out the door.

"Sergeant." Warner Conway stood in the doorway to his office. "There were six army men killed in that train raid. Six."

Cohen studied the message Bradshaw had given him, and nodded. "So there were." His jaw tightened.

"And I got excited about the *payroll.*"

"Figgers," drawled Sergeant Cohen. "Things are comin' from so many directions these days, a man hardly knows which way to jump. Patrols all over. Lieutenant Kincaid ambushed . . ."

Sergeant Breckenridge rode in with Weasel, Champlain, Trouble Thompson, Enright, and the scout, Turning Wind. They joined Lieutenant Smaldoon in front of the orderly room and then rode back out.

A few hours later they were standing a short distance from the holdup site, watching Turning Wind prowl among the dead cow carcasses.

Turning Wind finally wrapped up his examination and returned to the squad. "Men dragging steers from tracks covered sign. Steers killed with Cheyenne arrows."

Smaldoon was wearing his Indian-killing look, but Breckenridge wondered, "You're buyin' it, Wind? You're sure they was Injuns? Cheyenne?"

Turning Wind shrugged helplessly. "No sign."

"Go look again."

"Sergeant—" Smaldoon interrupted.

"If you don't mind, sir, there's gotta be *somethin'*. Wind, go look again, all over, and see if you see *anything* that looks Injun."

Turning Wind did as he was told, with Mr. Smaldoon growing impatient, as if the thieving murderers were just over the near ridge and about to escape.

Turning Wind came back. "Nothing."

"Now are you happy, Sergeant?" said Smaldoon, an edge to his voice.

"Start trailin', Wind," said Sergeant Breckenridge.

They started off at a slow pace. Eight miles later, to the east, they stopped. The tracks they'd been following had joined a wagon road that ran north and south.

"Where's that lead?" asked Smaldoon, pointing south.

"Rock Creek."

"And the other way?"

"Couple of towns. Morgan's Hollow. Stilwell."

Turning Wind had already examined the far side of the road and had found no continuing sign.

"What about Indian villages?" pressed Lieutenant Smaldoon.

"Any number, I guess," answered Breckenridge. "Far's I know, they keep movin' around. Think they're still chasin' the buffalo. Ain't chasin' nothin'. Nothin' but a dream..."

Smaldoon was suddenly fed up with Breckenridge's homely philosophizing. "Well? Which way should we go?"

"Got me, sir. Looks like a clean getaway—"

"Sergeant!"

"Unless you want to split up, go both ways, look for sign leavin' the trail. Might get lucky, then again, might not, might be out here all summer. I figger the money ain't no good to an Injun, or to *anyone*, unless he spends it. Whyn't we jes' wait to see who's got money?"

Smaldoon nodded, accepting the advice reluctantly, gracelessly. Obviously he'd gotten his battlefield commission through fighting, not thinking.

Breckenridge, though, for all his rustic Southern mountaineer's ways and occasional taste for simpleminded homilies, *could* think, and on the way back to Outpost Number Nine he thought about it a lot, and decided that the chances of its having been Indians raiding that train were pretty damn slim. Not to leave one itty-bitty footprint behind in the dirt? Nothing? Not very likely. Or, as his granddaddy used to say . . .

Damn! What *did* his granddaddy used to say? Hell, he'd been out on these plains too goddamn long. Brains froze in winter, baked in summer, an' goddamn lieutenants who used to be sergeants and ought to *know* goddamn better.

Damn! Fine time fer Matt Kincaid to take himself a vacation.

twenty _____

Mulberry hadn't changed at all since Matt Kincaid had last seen him at Easy, save that he was now a corporal.

"Corporal's pay is better, sir, but it's still not enough. Pam does a lot of seamstress work, though."

"How *is* Pam?"

"Fine. Pregnant." He looked sheepish. It wasn't a comfortable topic. At one time, Matt himself had taken a go at Pamela, definitely unmarried at the time, while Mulberry was still fiddling around the edges. Matt hadn't known of Mulberry's interest, or else he would have forsworn the pleasure.

"So, the Mulberry tree bears fruit."

"Please, sir, I've had enough of that particular joke. Just hope the brat's mine." But if there was indeed some question, he appeared to be taking it well. He changed the subject. "Well, sir, what brings you by?"

"You've heard about the Crow jumping?"

"Yessir. I was down there just a few days before they took off. Sure didn't look very agitated to me."

"Did you happen to see a breed or mulatto hanging around?" Mulberry stared at him, then smiled. "I'll be damned . . . sir."

"You *did* see one?"

"No. But there's historical precedent. There was once a mountaineer, part American, part French, and part Negro. He talked the Crow into thinking he was really one of them, a Crow half-breed at the very least. He joined them and eventually became a chief. The *big* chief, according to him, but

140

then he was the one telling the story, and there are those that say Beckwith, or Beckwourth—that was his name, Jim Beckwith—was about the biggest liar in the entire West. And if you read this book he dictated, it has him leading two thousand Crow against fifteen hundred Blackfoot and making off with two thousand horses." Mulberry smiled. "He tended to exaggerate. But aside from that, actual numbers and such, the book's supposed to be pretty accurate, and valuable in understanding the Crow."

"This was a book?" asked Matt. "Published?"

"Yessir."

"And someone could have read it?"

"Naturally, sir. Anytime after the mid-fifties, I guess."

Matt Kincaid thought it over. "Fredericksburg, Virginia, the twenty-sixth of April."

Mulberry was silent as his brow knit. His skinny frame, upon which the army blue hung badly, was still. "Ah. Of course. That, I believe, sir, was when Beckwith was born. One of—"

"Thirteen children," Matt completed.

"That's right," said Mulberry, puzzled.

"And 1866?"

"That's when he died. He'd sort of retired, but was sent on a peace mission to the Crow. A feast was prepared. He died. Legend has it he was poisoned in order to keep his strength forever with the Crow Nation. No way of verifying that, of course. And he *was* pretty old at the time."

"We found some hides with 'JB' cut in them."

"When he was hunting and trapping with the Crow, he often put his initials on the hides, signifying they were his, especially if he was leaving them cached somewhere. Let me tell you, sir, ol' Jim turned a pretty penny as chief of the Crow, if he *was* chief of the Crow."

"Bloody Arm? Medicine Calf?"

Mulberry nodded. "He had a whole raft of names. The Indian tends to do that, and Beckwith especially. Those two names were the last ones Beckwith took. Medicine Calf represented the ultimate—" Ed Mulberry smiled. "Have you got yourself another mulatto Crow war chief, sir?"

"Yeah, we've got one. And a damn good fighter, too. Smart. Ex-army." A pained expression crossed Matt's face. "Thought I could round them up with a small patrol. Couldn't.

But then, I didn't know ahead of time that Barrett was leading them."

"Who, sir?"

"Errr, Medicine Calf." Matt almost blushed.

"Well, sir, if he's Medicine Calf now, then maybe you won't have too long to worry. Beckwith headed off for Florida soon after that. Then he came back, stayed with the Crow awhile, I guess, then more or less retired. Went west, far west."

"We lost this bunch headed southwest down through Idaho. Couldn't figure out where they were headed."

Mulberry nodded slowly.

"Now remember, Corporal, this guy's loony."

"Still, if he's following the book . . ."

"You got this book, Corporal?"

"I can get it, sir, but I don't need it to tell you where he's heading."

Billy Caber opened the cupboard and saw bottle upon bottle. "Which one?"

"Any one," said his mother softly. "Any will do, they're all the same . . . the *best*."

Must be. They all had labels for a change. The bottles had never had labels before.

His mother, still lying in bed though it was past noon, poured herself a glassful and then sipped from it.

Her head fell back. "Tired," she said, "so tired."

"Where'd the bottles come from, Ma?"

"Your pa bought them. That way he can just forget about me. It keeps me happy . . . he's right . . ."

But Billy figured there was something wrong with that. His mother had weakened considerably in the past month. She'd cough most of the night. She'd always coughed a lot, ugly, wracking sounds, making Billy want to stay away from home. But now the coughing was worse.

He listened to her have a coughing siege, her thin body shaking.

The doc came every few weeks, but all he seemed to do was sit around sharing booze with her. He'd probably be showing up all the time now that they had labeled booze.

His mother, on those visits, would always take out the old photographs of herself, taken way back when she lived down in Memphis. They showed what a lovely woman she'd once been, with fine, delicate features. She'd tell the doctor how in those days she'd been the admiration of every man that saw her.

But once the doctor was gone she'd tell Billy, still in the spirit of reminiscence, how the attention had passed considerably beyond admiration.

"Billy," she'd sigh, "you wouldn't believe how they longed to look on this body of mine, this poor thing that it's become..." Another sip. "Why, boy, they'd pay money, good money and lots of it, just to stroke this flesh, and do a lot more, too.... Oh, your mother was a beauty, boy, a real beauty."

Billy believed it. He could still see the ghost of that beauty.

"And I was already married, Billy." She smiled, as if at the ridiculous wonder of that.

"To Pa?"

"To Pa. At least I *think* he's your pa." She smiled, eyeing him, her watery eyes seeming to hold deeper, even crueler, revelations. "Have you seen your pa lately, Billy?"

"Not fer a while."

"Probably did and didn't recognize him. He'll be the man in the fancy clothes drinking and gambling. He always loved to gamble...."

For a moment Billy thought he'd wandered into the wrong home, or into a fairy story, or...

"But you do look like me, Billy, you surely do...even though you're awfully little...like a little girl. You're strong, though, aren't you? Strong...and brave. Come here, Billy."

He came and she took hold of a pinch of skin and squeezed. He could have pulled away easily, but didn't.

She pinched harder, as hard as she could. "You don't mind it, Billy, do you, the pain? Like your ma's got pain."

She couldn't pinch as hard anymore, hardly hurt at all, but tears came to Billy's eyes.

"No, ma, I don't mind."

Later, Billy looked into the Full House Saloon.

There his father was, gambling like a fool, throwing money around like there was no end to it.

Billy didn't approve of such goings-on, especially with his mother the way she was.

143

Bull Caber saw Billy standing in the doorway, watching him.

His eyes narrowed for a second, but that was all. He might have been looking at a stranger.

twenty-one ━━━━━━━━━

Matt Kincaid got back to Outpost Number Nine not long after Chubb had arrived with the living, the dead, and the wounded.

"Did you go visit Corporal Mulberry, Matt?" Captain Conway asked soon after he'd ridden in.

"Yes. From some stuff Barrett yelled—"

"It is Barrett, then? Windy said something about that. Have to admit, it sounded strange."

"It still sounds strange. But it was that unexpected thing you were thinking about when you sent me out. Sorry I didn't do a better job."

"It happens, Matt."

"Anyway, I figured we were dealing with a madman, but crazy like a fox. I thought Mulberry might be able to help me out. And he did. I've put together a sort of theory. Barrett not only thinks he's a real, honest-to-goodness Crow war chief, but a reborn Jim Beckwith."

"That Crow mulatto?"

"The same. The idea had occurred to me, but I needed confirmation. Mulberry gave it. And I also figured that if Mulberry could tell me what the real Beckwith did, we might get a lead on what Barrett's up to."

"And?"

"Beckwith headed for California. Without the Crow, incidentally—he'd left them by then—but I figure Barrett's kind of condensing everything. Anyway, he headed for California, found a pass through the mountains, and the pass is still named for him, Beckwith Pass, about twenty-five miles north of Reno, on the California border. And there's a Beckwith Peak and a town of Beckwith to boot. So he headed for California and settled for a while in the Feather River Valley. That's sort of north central, around Yuba City, Marysville. I figure *that's* where our friend Barrett, goddamned Bloody Arm Medicine Calf, is headed."

Captain Conway blinked at him. "He's really gotten you worked up, hasn't he?"

"I lost eight men, sir, *eight*, mostly due to that idiot Plowright. Barrett waved a white woman's ass in his face and it was like flapping a red flag in front of a bull. Charged his men right into a goddamned ambush."

"Incidentally, Matt, did you know that bulls are *not* enraged by the sight of a red flag?"

"Hm?"

"No. It's *cows* that are maddened by red flags. *Bulls* are enraged at being mistaken for a cow."

Matt stared at Captain Conway, his mouth hanging open. Conway realized he'd picked the wrong time to launch his little joke. "But I know how you feel, Matt. And it's too bad Plowright was one of the survivors . . . if you can call him a survivor."

Matt nodded. He didn't want to talk about it. It was never easy for men to discuss another man's getting his balls shot off. And, Jesus, Captain Conway might even try to make a joke about *that*, too. So instead, Matt told the captain of the wires he'd sent west, wires that warned of the coming of Barrett and the Crow. Then he asked, "Anything happen while I was gone?"

"Anything *happen*?" Where should he start? "Well, to sum it up, we've been running around like crazy, trying to *save* Mr. Lo. Around here it's been the *whites* on the warpath. Remember Many Sons? Wanted you to be a godfather to one of his recent offspring?"

Matt smiled. "That old rooster's going to screw himself to death."

"Not hardly." And then Captain Conway told Matt of Many Sons' fate, and of all the rest that had happened.

"Anyone told Plowright what happened to his wife?"

"I hope not. *I* certainly haven't. Damn, I had it all set to ship Plowright and Clara out the moment he got here."

146

"Sounds like you had a real problem there."

"Hope I did right. But hell, Matt, you can't hang some men for jumping on a woman who's been teasing them *and* stealing from them. On the other hand, I know damn well some of those men would hump a she-buffalo, given the chance."

"Who's nursing him?"

"Maggie and Flora sometimes, but Clara mostly. Seems to be doing all right, too. Plowright's not complaining, anyway. Sergeant Rothausen looks in too, occasionally. Changes the dressing. But that's not working out so well." Captain Conway made a face that was half-unpleasant, half-amused. "When you consider the particular area of the body he's working on, and what Plowright's missing . . . well, every time Dutch serves up something similar to the men, like that sausage he sometimes makes, you can imagine the comments that get bandied about."

Night had fallen. Maggie looked up as Clara entered the Plowright quarters.

"Weren't sure you were ever coming back," Maggie joked, though it wasn't really a joke.

"It's a beautiful night out," said Clara.

Ernest Plowright rolled his head in her direction and smiled. "I'll bet it is, Clara, near as beautiful as the most beautiful girl in all of Missouri."

"I'll be going now," said Maggie. "If you need any help, come a-runnin'. He may need his bandages changed. He's still bleeding some."

Clara said with mock severity, "If he'd just stay quiet."

"You make a man want to move, Clara."

Clara nodded gamely. Now that he can't *do* anything, he starts sounding like a real Romeo.

Maggie left.

"Well, no matter what it is you may want to do, Ernest, just don't do it. We've got to get you all healed."

"Don't worry, Clara. With you by my side, I'll be well in no time. Yep, I can feel myself healin' right now, practically feel the juices flowing."

What he did feel was a trickle of blood running from his groin, soaking into the sheets. It had been a damn difficult sewing job, that done in Virginia City by a surgeon who'd had his baptism in the War. And in the War they very rarely sewed, mostly just chopped.

147

"Can't wait till I'm up and about, Clara, get to stand and wrap my arms around you."

Damn. It was driving her crazy.

But it was true, not just her imagination. Plowright's wound, his emasculation, had left him a new man, paradoxically a very masculine man, if only in spirit. No longer was his sexuality in constant conflict with whatever it was that repressed him, suppressed him, held him in a puritanical grip. No longer did he have to question, examine, analyze, suspect, and censure everything involving the two sexes; no longer did he have to make those hard choices. He was finally a free man.

"Clara, I know you're wondering about the future, what we'll do. A family... children.... Well, don't you worry. My own family, they got a big ol' farm just waitin' for me, for me and *you*. It's been waitin' for years. My folks wanted me to take it over a long time ago. But I had to get away for a while. My folks, they're kind of strong, strict, churchgoin' types. I had to get away. But now, I figure that part of my life, that there rebellion, that's over with." But, sadly, something about his manner, his voice, his eyes, showed that he knew the rebellion had never taken place. "No, I figure I can handle my folks, handle them and their funny ideas. Y'know, they remind me of Medford sometimes."

Clara shuddered.

"So the farm's there, and it's a good farm, and we can adopt some kids, or..." He sighed deeply.

"Now, Clara, don't you take this wrong, but... I figger you're a woman, a *real* woman, and a real woman wants to, *you* know, *do* things, things I can't do... and she wants to have her own children. Well, we won't be too far from Saint Lou... and maybe you'd like to visit there a few times... and maybe someday you'll come back carryin' a baby inside you. Now listen, listen. My folks don't have to know I'm hurt the way I am. No one does. You understand, Clara? You understand?

She looked at him with soft eyes. "I understand, Ernest." Why couldn't he have been like this before? "I understand."

"Aw, hell, Clara, call me Blowhard. Everybody else does." And he grinned.

She took his hand and sat by his bed.

After a while he reached out and laid his hand against her breast. "Feels nice. Real nice. You're shaped real nice, Clara."

148

Tears came to Clara's eyes.

When they'd finally dried, she asked her husband if he'd mind if she left him for a little while, to get some air and think things over.

"I don't mind," he said.

"But don't you move," she told him. "Just lie there and maybe go to sleep."

His smile said that he would.

She stepped outside, closing the door quietly behind her. The night was as beautiful as she had said—cool, clear, glittering with stars, a large, warm, orange moon just coming up over the horizon. That moon would soon climb high, get small and turn cold white, but for the moment it was a comforting, friendly presence.

Clara climbed the parapet, to the sod roofing atop the housing. Some guard would probably challenge her and, if he was a stickler for rules, try to kick her off. But she didn't care.

Clara wandered along the guard post along the south wall. She could hear the company's horses milling restlessly down below her. She leaned against the parapet and stared over it to the south, thinking of Plowright's words, his plans.

Sergeant Plowright was thirsty. The water pitcher was at the far side of the room, on the dresser.

Damned dresser looked like it had been through *all* the wars, all the way back to the Revolution.

He needed water. Should he yell? Was Clara standing just outside, taking the air? Or had she wandered off? Had she gone to meet someone?

Old habits die hard, and Plowright felt a spasm of jealousy. Thoughts and words—"You can do as you like, Clara"—weren't the same as emotions.

He lay back until he had his agitation under control. And then he set out to get the water. Hell, no reason why he shouldn't be able to do *that*. Dutch thought he was healing up pretty good. Probably as good as his other wounds, and they hardly hurt at all. He wasn't sure exactly what had happened in his crotch, but hell, he'd only lost a few things he hadn't had a hell of a lot of use for. It was like losing a finger, or even an arm; they usually healed up pretty neat.

Plowright rolled carefully from the bed, stood upright, took two unsteady steps toward the dresser, and then started to pitch forward dizzily, his goddamn legs not working at all.

He went down over a footstool, reaching still for the water pitcher.

He missed the water pitcher, but got the dresser, which finally collapsed, bringing the water pitcher spilling down over him.

"Damn," he muttered, drenched. "Damn," he said again, adjusting his position on the packed sod floor. "Damn," he said a third time, still not feeling all that comfortable, but thinking maybe he'd just lie there until Clara got back. She'd probably make a big scene. He sort of anticipated her fussing over him. Except he *was* drenched. He could still feel the water trickling off him. Probably catch pneumonia to go along with everything else.

But only if he was lucky. The work the Virginia City doctor had done on Plowright had been tricky because one of the main arteries of the leg, the femoral, had nearly been severed. He'd sewed it up as best he could, reducing the flow of blood to a trickle.

But the sewing job had been just barely adequate. Left undisturbed for a few weeks, it might finally have healed, resealing itself.

But it was the femoral artery that had come apart when Plowright went down. The 'water" he felt trickling was blood. And the reason he didn't find himself lying in a pool of blood, which might have led to some lusty, lifesaving shouts, was because of the sod floor. It was hardpacked, but it still soaked up the life juice.

Clara was giving her future life with Sergeant Plowright a lot of thought, and it was beginning to look brighter just as the moon was beginning to look brighter. Ernest could work, tend the farm, make it a success. She'd help, take her weekends in town as an unmarried woman, or possibly even a widow lady, and enjoy herself. And maybe she would bring Ernest back the baby he seemed to want.

If she'd known Ernest was going to be such a strange man, she would have thought a lot before marrying him. But maybe it was going to work out.

She heard the guard being changed. How long had she been up here? The moon sure was high.

She found her way to a ladder and climbed down to the

150

parade. She'd barely touched ground when she found Maggie Cohen standing by her side.

"What were you doing up there?" It was late and Maggie was tired, but her voice was crisp.

"Thinking. About Ernest, Ernest and me. It's going to be all right, Maggie. Me and Ernie, we worked it out, it's going to be fine."

"Did you tell him anything about what happened to you? Get him excited?"

"Oh, no. I'm never going to tell him about that. Why? Somebody told him? Y'all *promised*."

"You shouldn't have left." Maggie's voice was no longer crisp.

"I wasn't . . . I wasn't gone for *long*."

"He tried to get up for something. Fell down. His wound opened. It was an artery, one of the big ones. Dammit, Clara, he wasn't supposed to move at all."

"So? Is he all right?"

"He's dead. He bled to death."

Clara looked to the heavens. The moon was white and bright now, and very cold.

twenty-two _____

Colonel Black Jack Pratt, commander of the regiment headquartered at Fort Churchill, had had his run-ins with the Paiute, the Shoshone, the Bannock. He gave no quarter and expected none.

Ten minutes after the telegraph message had reached him, the message warning of the probable Crow descent on California, Colonel Pratt was bent over his maps.

Fort Churchill lay about twenty miles east of Virginia City—Nevada's Virginia City—which itself was another twenty or so miles east of Lake Tahoe and the California border.

The usual route into California, the California Trail, angled southwesterly some fifteen to twenty miles north of Fort Churchill, following the Truckee River, which came down out of Pyramid Lake. Anyone crossing from Nevada to California might be expected to use that route. But not, according to the message, these particular Crow. The Crow, apparently, were following a vision rather than a trail, and that particular vision was going to take them through Beckwith Pass—if they came at all. Through Beckwith Pass and on to the Feather River Valley.

Well, if Black Jack Pratt had anything to say about it, they wouldn't get beyond Beckwith Pass.

Beckwith Pass was about another thirty miles northwest, beyond the California Trail. It may not have been the best route through the mountains, but it had been Beckwith's very own, and he'd been proud of it.

Colonel Pratt knew Beckwith Pass well. It was there

152

he would cut those red bastards down.

Pratt, who commanded both cavalry and dragoon outfits, chose the dragoons, the Twelfth Mounted Infantry, to meet the renegade Crow at Beckwith Pass; the cavalry he would save for possible desert skirmishes.

The Twelfth's various components were scattered about the high desert, some closer to Beckwith Pass than to Fort Churchill, but Pratt decided to take care of this action himself. There were going to be no survivors, and for that he didn't trust his company commanders. *They* all thought Mr. Lo was on the run, beaten, cowed, and they were wont to be merciful. Black Jack Pratt knew better.

He mounted up the First Platoon of the Twelfth's Headquarters Company, a grumbling bunch of men, used to letting the various regimental outposts handle the dirty work, and led them out at dawn one morning.

They rode all day and reached Beckwith Pass by late afternoon. The scouts told Colonel Pratt there'd been no Indians of any consequential numbers through the pass in recent weeks.

Pratt deployed his men and told them to be prepared for a long wait.

"What about sleeping?" asked Lieutenant Powell, the platoon leader, a vicious officer quite to Pratt's liking.

"In relays. They may come through at night." In fact he hoped they did come through at night.

"It'll make it hard to separate the white hostages from the hostiles," commented Powell, not really giving a damn.

Pratt smiled, then lied. "I sent a query. They left the women up in Idaho, had them a shootout up there, some jackass first looie got himself wiped out. That isn't about to happen here."

Colonel Pratt was the kind of man who thought Chivington was one of the West's great heroes.

It wouldn't be long now, thought Barrett, riding at the head of his twenty-odd men.

There had been losses along the way: wounds that had gone into infection; a poisonous water hole (such had been their luck that the dead carcasses and skeletons littering the area had recently been hauled off by an enterprising crowd bent on making a profit on the bones and horns); an ill-advised skirmish with a small wagon train loaded with sharpshooters. The farther west they went, the weaker his medicine seemed to get.

153

He had Alicia, though, and the boy, for his retirement in the Feather River Valley. Many brave Barrett warriors loomed on the distant horizon, drawn from Alicia's belly. They would be wise, his children, wise in the ways of *all* races.

The only problem, though, with Alicia and the boy, was that they weren't terribly bright—which might have accounted for why she hadn't tried to slit his throat. But beyond that, he'd told her of his vision and she'd not seemed terribly impressed. In fact, of late both she and the boy had been hanging close to Lame Dog. She might even be sleeping with his second-in-command.

So to hell with it. Medicine Calf was above fretting over such petty domestic trifles. When he had to, he made do with the other girl, Mary, despite her constant sniffling and weeping. Perhaps Mary would eventually bear his children. Her body was strong.

The sun was setting ahead of them, sinking into the cleft that was Beckwith Pass. Still some miles and hours away, the distance was deceptive. They'd be there by nightfall and cross in the darkness. The moon would be up late, but it would be best not to wait for it and proceed in blackness. He didn't know how wide the pass was, but it didn't look too wide. Fine for an ambush. But if there was anyone looking for them going into California, they would surely be waiting farther south, flanking Donner's route.

Four hours later, in pitch blackness, they gained the pass and started through. Barrett, his improved horsemanship notwithstanding, dropped back to the rear of the column, joined by Lame Dog, Alicia, the boy, and weepish Mary. Buffalo Hump, keen-eyed and a single entity with his pony, a veritable centaur, was up front leading the way.

"They're coming," whispered the scout to Colonel Pratt.

"How many?"

"No see. Too dark. I listen and count maybe twenty, thirty...."

"Can't see a goddamn thing," said Mr. Powell. "They might have some white prisoners with them." He wasn't quite *that* vicious and was having second thoughts. "Might have picked them up since you got that wire."

"And what would *you* do, Mr. Powell?" demanded Colonel Pratt fiercely.

154

"Maybe let them pass, stay in touch until daybreak."

"And have them spread out and disappear all over California? You're mad . . . or maybe you aren't fit to be an officer in my command."

"Failing that, sir," said Powell, "I'd station a man, a scout maybe, fifty yards back. He starts firing when he's sure the last hostile's passed by, and then we open fire."

"*Now* you're thinking, mister."

Powell wasn't too happy with that "thinking," but dammit, there was a career at stake. And any white man stupid enough to let himself get taken hostage by these hostiles pretty much deserved what he got.

But he also knew that Black Jack Pratt had sent no follow-up query. So he quit thinking about it.

Colonel Pratt's scout had sharp ears, but they weren't quite sharp enough. Or maybe it was just that the deeper Barrett rode into the pitch-black cleft, the deeper grew his foreboding. And, unconsciously, he let the space grow between himself (and Lame Dog, Alicia, Mary, and the boy) and the rest of the single file of Crow. And the scout didn't hear them bringing up the far rear. Thus it was that the scout's signal shots, which took Spotted Elk off his pony and triggered the unholy rain of fire that decimated the rest of the band, brought Barrett's group up short and had them spinning their mounts and crashing pell-mell back down the trail.

By some grace, none of their horses collided and none went down.

And the tumult to his rear made Barrett think of a Gatling gun, so thunderous and constant was the roar. But he knew it wasn't. The Devil himself wouldn't have been able to haul a full Gatling, near half a ton, up that trail.

But a Gatling couldn't have made more of a bloody shambles.

They came out of the pass back onto the high desert and rode east, rode like fury, rode like that very Devil with his Gatling was hot on their heels.

155

twenty-three _____

    "They got 'em!" cried Four Eyes Bradshaw, turning away from the telegraph.

"Got who?" asked Sergeant Cohen, as Matt Kincaid came wandering out of his office.

"The Crow. Colonel Pratt and the Twelfth nailed them right where Matt—err, Lieutenant Kincaid said they would, Beckwith Pass."

"Let me see that, Corporal," said Matt, and then he studied the message. "Twenty-three dead." He frowned. "Get back on that wire, Corporal. I want to know if *any* got away. And give them a description of Barrett. I want to know for sure they got *him*."

"Feeling a little mean, sir?" Cohen asked over the telegraph's clacking.

"No," said Matt, "but it sounds too easy, too neat. It was real dark last night, and that's not a well-traveled trail. Barrett wouldn't have been out front."

"Second or third, then. It was *his* war party. Chiefs don't ride at the rear."

Matt smiled sadly. "Old Bloody Arm wasn't your regular chief. I just can't believe he'd ride straight into a trap like that. Something would save him. Luck. Medicine."

"Sounds like you like him, sir. Miss him, anyways."

"Oh, hell, Sergeant, the man's crazy. You can't hate a crazy man, but one who's crazy like Barrett is . . . you're crazy yourself if you don't fear him a little."

The exchange of telegraph messages between Outpost Number Nine and Fort Churchill, by way of any number of intermediary stations, took all morning and much of the afternoon; but when it was done, Matt Kincaid was fairly certain that Barrett/Bloody Arm/Medicine Calf was out there somewhere, still alive.

But where?

That afternoon the dispatch rider from regimental HQ rode in carrying various orders and the usual literature disseminated by the War Department (often it consisted of some "special" knowledge concerning Indian ways that had been common knowledge to field commanders for months, if not years). He also brought a package for Matt Kincaid.

"It's a book," exclaimed Matt, opening the package. It was a dog-eared volume, not new. "Well, I'll be damned. It's the Beckwith book, the one Barrett's been trying to follow." It was a thick book and was going to take time to read.

Sergeant Cohen, Captain Conway, and Corporal Bradshaw regarded him silently. Matt was not known to spend much time reading.

A several-page note accompanied the volume. Matt read it, then said, "Seems the book ends with Beckwith in California, but that wasn't where he stayed. Mulberry's got an account here of his movements. He went back to Missouri, then back out to Denver with a load of something for an old friend. Got married there for a while, then he lived with an Indian girl named Sue, somewhere around there. Used to get visited by Crow all the time, reliving the good old days." Matt smiled. "Got arrested for receiving stolen goods. That was in '63. Then in '64 he shot and killed some colored man, a blacksmith, got off on self-defense. Must have been pretty old by then. Hell—" He did some quick arithmetic. "Sixty-six he was. . . . Then . . . Jesus Christ! He was one of the scouts for Chivington at Sand Creek when that son of a bitch—"

"Lieutenant!" barked Captain Conway.

"—wiped out Black Kettle's people. Dammit, sir, you know those Cheyenne only wanted peace."

Warner Conway said nothing, merely compressed his lips.

157

"Wonder what Beckwith thought about that?" mused Matt. "Guess he didn't care for the Cheyenne, but still . . ."

Matt flipped to the final pages of the book and scanned them silently for a while. Then, finally he said, "Well, I'll be damned. Some big friend of the red man Beckwith was. Right at the end here he outlines his plan for *exterminating* the red man. Demoralize and weaken them with whiskey, leaving them prey to other bands and reducing their numbers that way. And then send a select troop of mountaineers in to destroy the buffalo, starve the Indian, and kill what they couldn't starve. . . ."

Matt stared down at the printed page.

"Seems to me," said Sergeant Cohen, "in one way or another, that's about what we *are* doing."

"Mulberry says this information on Beckwith isn't any big secret." Matt thought about that for a moment. "I guess he's suggesting that Barrett might know all this stuff too. Figures. Seems like he made a pretty good study of Beckwith." Matt slipped the note into the book and closed it with finality.

"Well, Matt?" Warner Conway asked.

"Well what, sir? I'm not going to *read* this book, if that's what you're wondering, not unless I get shot and laid up for a month. What I—" His attention was drawn to something out in the parade. "What's the ambulance doing here?"

An ambulance was a light, well-sprung, comfortable, canvas-topped wagon. It was used, when necessary, to transport the wounded and ailing, but more often was used like any other wagon. It was preferred, in fact, by ladies for its easy-riding qualities.

"Pickin' up the Plowright woman," said Sergeant Cohen. "With Blowhard buried, there ain't much sense in keepin' *her* around. Funny thing is, though, she was about as broke up over his dyin' as any woman I've ever seen. And now she's headin' back to live with his folks, can you beat that?"

"Women are sure funny creatures," muttered Bradshaw, and they all stared at him. Four Eyes was perhaps the least qualified on the post to make any such judgment. "'Least, that's what I *hear*, anyway."

"Well, Corporal, you hear right," said Matt, "and I'm glad you reminded me that you're here. I want you to send me a message."

"Send *you* a message? . . . Sir?"

158

"*For* me, Four Eyes. Damn, you're too clever by half some-times. Take this down. 'To Deputy U.S. Marshal Long, care of U.S. Marshal Vail, First District Court of Colorado. Message as follows..."

The day slid easily into midafternoon. The white violence against Mr. Lo had abated, dampened considerably by Easy's unrelenting patrols, to say nothing of the swift, deadly counterattacks led by Lieutenants Allison and Price (though Price was quick to pass the credit on to Sergeant Olsen). The only matter hanging fire was that concerning Mr. Smaldoon, Sergeant Breckenridge, and the train robbery. So far, no Indians had been seen throwing enormous amounts of money around. Nor had any whites, or at least no such doings had been reported.

Smaldoon still thought they should have stuck to the trail once they'd been on it. Breckenridge, privately, said that Smaldoon's commission had gone to his head and turned his brain into standard officer mush.

"Weasel. You got a visitor."

A visitor? There he was, sitting in the sun outside the barracks, and some joker comes up and says he has a visitor? "Where?"

The messenger, one of the guard mount, indicated the front gate. Weasel followed him there.

Billy Caber stood outside the gate, a ratty-looking horse by his side.

"Whyn't you let him in?"

"Ain't supposed to."

"Hey, the gal's gone, Blowhard's dead, an' you don't see me or the rest doin' hard labor anymore, do you?"

"Orders."

Weasel looked around. The officer of the day, Lieutenant Allison, had just stepped out of the guard house.

"Mr. Allison, sir..." Allison stopped, looked. "Kin you let Billy Caber in, sir? They ain't no more reason to keep him out."

"Why, Private?"

" 'Cause...'cause he's my friend."

Mr. Allison spent about two minutes mentally reviewing

159

the entire case, down to its most minute ramifications. "Oh, hell, why not."

Back in front of the barracks, sunning himself again, Gillies asked, "How's yer ma?"

"She ain't good," said Billy. "She's gettin' worse, an' she's always drinkin' and sayin' funny things..."

"Like what?"

" 'Bout me, mostly... like who I am, really."

"Who *are* you?"

But Billy wasn't saying. "Then Pa, he's come into a whole bunch o' money, buys her all the booze she needs, or *wants,* anyway. Good booze too, got real labels...but he don't do nothin' else for her.... He loves her, I *know* he loves her"—his fierceness brought doubt onto Weasel's face more plainly—"or I guess he does, but he's lettin' her die. Him and his buddies, they all got money now, hang around the Full House, playin' and drinkin' and...and foolin' with them *women....*"

Gillies' eyes were closed, but he was thinking. Boy, was he thinking. Goddamn! God-Almighty-damn! Finally he said, "C'mon, Billy, let's go visit."

He marched himself and Billy to the orderly room.

"Private Gillies and Billy Caber requestin' permission to talk to Lieutenant Kincaid, Sergeant...or Mr. Smaldoon, maybe, iffen he's around...."

Cohen eyed him wearily. It was damned hot. Then he turned his gaze on Billy. "What's *he* doing on the post? I thought—"

"Send 'em in, Sergeant," came Matt's voice from his office. "Can't kick the kid out till the sun cools off some, anyway."

Weasel Gillies ushered Billy Caber into Matt's office and threw up a salute, his usual one that looked like his arm was broken in about ten places. Billy Caber, though, snapped a regulation salute up so smartly and breezily that Matt felt a soft rush of air. "Who the hell recruited *him*?" he asked, smiling.

Though Billy's salute amazed Weasel as much as Matt, he left that aside and said, "Heard Sergeant Breckenridge say how you was lookin' for a whole lot of money suddenly showin' up. Well, tell 'im, Billy."

"Tell 'im? That's my pa I was talkin' about."

Matt eyed the two of them. Then he said softly, "I understand you want to be a soldier, Billy."

"I ain't old enough," said Billy in a flat voice.

"You will be soon enough. And folks can put in a good word. Private Gillies, here, even though he doesn't know how to salute, is pretty well respected"—Weasel almost fell down—"and my word carries some weight. Now what's this all about?"

Matt Kincaid rode out with Lieutenant Smaldoon, Sergeant Breckenridge, and Privates Gillies, Champlain, Enright, Thompson, the recovered Moore, and Billy Caber. They'd gotten Billy a horse that could keep up.

"We'd have reached Morgan's Hollow if we'd gone north along that wagon road," Mr. Smaldoon pointed out to Sergeant Breckenridge after they were under way.

"And what, sir? We'd have found them runnin' around in Injun clothes celebratin' the robbery?"

Kincaid was bothered by the exchange. "Remember, we have no proof as yet. We've got to find some evidence. The money bags, maybe. Or the money itself. We're in luck there, since the stuff came straight from the mint, all nicely numbered in order. If we find some of them, we'll know we've hit pay dirt."

"What if these jokers hit a bank instead?" asked Breckenridge.

"That's the law's problem," said Matt. "We'll let 'em buy us some drinks, give 'em a head start, and then let a U.S. Marshal in on the big secret."

They rode into Morgan's Hollow, making no effort to appear inconspicuous. Any number of townsfolk, including those in the Full House Saloon, saw them and wondered what they were doing there.

They tied up in the street before the saloon above which the Cabers lived. A few of the men misdirected attention by stomping noisily into the saloon, while Kincaid, Smaldoon, Breckenridge, Gillies, and Billy Caber slipped up the stairs to the Caber rooms.

Billy's mom was lying on her bed, a bottle and a glass on the floor beside it. She was lying on her back. Her nightgown, once white, now gray, was pulled all the way up and over her head.

"Ma!" cried Billy, and his jaw started quivering as Breckenridge took an iron hold on him.

Matt approached the bed. The gray-white flesh barely covered her bones. Most of the hair had fallen out of where it should have been. Matt pulled the gown down to cover her. Then he stared into her eyes, which were open.

The face had fine bones, but that was all. Her hair looked like she'd brushed it recently. And then he saw the brush lying by her head.

Matt felt Billy Caber by his side. Billy was holding his mother's hand. "Your hands are *cold*, Ma."

Matt slowly turned away from the dead woman. "Have a look around," he said.

They searched, and high in the back of a cupboard they found a money pouch with bundles of money still inside.

"He *killed* her!"

Billy was looking at them, shriveled even smaller, shaking pitifully. "He killed her. *He* killed her." He shuddered with a long, drawn-out sob. "She said he wasn't my pa, my real pa. Someone *else* was my pa.... Weasel? Kill 'im, *please*? Kill 'im? For my ma?"

Matt Kincaid turned, intending to tell Gillies not to move an inch, not to go off half-cocked, but Gillies wasn't there.

Enright and the rest had drifted back on out of the saloon; there wasn't much to do in there if they weren't going to drink. They saw Gillies burst from the upstairs door, skitter down the rickety stairs, and hotfoot it on down the street. Naturally they were interested, and almost as naturally they trailed him, wondering what the hell had happened, and *was* happening, upstairs.

... Where Billy Caber was saying, "Weasel will get 'im."

"Weasel will get his goddamn head shot off," said Matt. "He's got more than one to deal with."

Billy's eyes suddenly widened and he ran from the room. Kincaid, Smaldoon, and Breckenridge almost fell over each other, chasing after him.

As it was, the rickety staircase collapsed under their weight. Smaldoon emerged from the wreckage hobbling, while the others were bruised but otherwise fit.

"Where the hell did that kid go? Where're the *men*?" Smaldoon yelled.

"Likely followed Gillies," Matt replied.

"Followed him *where*?" demanded Smaldoon.

Jesus, thought Matt, was he going to have to blow his nose for him?

"Me and Mr. Smaldoon'll take this side, sir," said Breckenridge, leaving the far side to Matt.

Matt guessed that Breck wanted the action for himself and figured this was the best side. Well, hell, why not, Breck deserved some fun.

Meanwhile, Gillies was edging along one inner wall of the Full House, his eyes on two men at the bar and four others at a nearby table. The six were paying very close attention to their drinks. Even though none had noticed Gillies enter—Weasel was so small that hardly anyone ever noticed him—they were all expecting something. They were all poised, still, like the cocked hammers of sixguns.

Gillies recognized one of the men at the bar as Bull Caber.

Caber must have sensed something. His eyes slowly swung around the room until they met Weasel's. Instant recognition.

Damn, thought Weasel, this wasn't the way it was supposed to be. He bent his knees slightly, subtly, lowering himself another inch or so. Those bastards were going to have to shoot through hardwood tables to get him.

"You boys better chuck it in," he drawled quietly—hell, he'd never in his life said "chuck it in," much less *drawled*, until he'd crossed that damned Mississippi. "We got the goods on yuh."

"You sittin' down, yuh bastard?" said one of the other men. "Whyn't yuh stand up where we kin see yuh?"

Now, that pissed Gillies off just a mite.

The saloon's batwing doors suddenly swung in and out, and little Billy Caber entered and stopped, breathing hard.

He looked at his pa, his face wearing an indecipherable expression.

Bull Caber looked right back at him, with no expression at all. He might have been looking at a stranger.

"*You* brung 'em," Bull Caber finally growled. "You little bastard. You know that? That yer a *bastard*? Yer effin' ma couldn't keep her legs closed, she'd spread 'em fer anyone." He read the hurt in the boy's face and grinned. "Like as not you got a nigger fer a pa."

"Don't, Pa!"

"But I was the last one she had, you better b'lieve thet."

"Don't!"

"An' now, yuh little bastard, you kin join her—"

Bull Caber's hand had already started sweeping the big Colt

up level before Weasel began his draw. But Gillies wasn't called Weasel for nothing; weasels are *quick*—and quiet.

And quiet he was as the Scoff whispered from its holster. Bull Caber did get a shot off, shooting right where a man's chest should have been—when you shoot that fast you shoot automatically, aim automatically, out of habit—and the slug whistled over Billy's head. All it accomplished was to go on out the door and take Buford Champlain's campaign hat out into the street, sending Buford digging for China.

And there was hardly time for an echo before Weasel Gillies started pumping slug after slug into Caber.

The slugs pinned Bull Caber to the bar until Weasel quit, and then Caber slid down into a heap on the floor.

Blood spread faster than the porous floorboards could soak it up.

"Pa!" Little Billy ran to the body of Bull Caber and fell down upon it, weeping.

And Gillies' mouth fell open.

Then a bullet whistling by sent him pitching to the floor, reaching for his second Scoff.

Caber's friends didn't figure they'd better waste time on a barroom shootout, especially with just one man. By the time they got him, the rest of the blue-legs would be pouring in. The time to *git*, if gittin' was to be done, was right then. So they lit out the back of the saloon.

. . . Where they ran into Sergeant Breckenridge and Private Buford Champlain.

Breckenridge, hearing the shots, had headed for the back alley without a moment's hesitation. Champlain, from his ground-level view, had seen him go and crawled after him; anything was better than getting your hat shot off by someone you couldn't even see.

But there they were, and he saw them plainly enough when they came out the back, waving their hoglegs. He put bullets into two of them before a third put one in him, ending his short and misspent life on the spot.

Breckenridge had unfortunately wasted his first two bullets on the same owlhoots Champlain had picked on—those two were dead before they knew they were being shot—and by the time he'd put meaningful holes in Champlain's killer, the other two had ducked back inside the saloon.

One of the three downed outlaws was still alive, gutshot

but breathing, and he might have made it. But Breckenridge looked down at Champlain's eyes, staring up at him lifelessly, then looked around to see who was looking—no one—and stepped over to the wounded man and blew his head off.

Calmly reloading, Breckenridge smiled down at his victim. "Bet you feel a whole lot better now, don't you? Kill a man— get killed. Kind of evens things up. Maybe the Lord'll take that into account."

He looked up at the sound of more firing from out front.

The two remaining outlaws had reentered the saloon, only to find it fast filling with soldiers. They threw their guns down immediately.

Weasel eyed them, frustrated. Smaldoon was as sore as a boil. And the rest felt the same, even the townsfolk who had no use for these wastrels.

Matt Kincaid came in from the street and pushed through the men to stand by Mr. Smaldoon. He saw what had happened. "Enright, Thompson, Moore," he said, "get on outside." He missed spotting Weasel.

The three privates left, wondering.

Matt then spoke to the two remaining outlaws. "All right, you boys pick those guns back up and stick 'em in your holsters."

Both of them stared at Matt and slowly shook their heads.

"Do it," Matt said. "They're littering up the floor. But do it *slowly*."

The two men looked at each other, then reached down and picked up their guns. One of them said, "I reckon you're the boss, Lieutenant, but you sure ain't gonna get us to draw on yuh."

"Put yours away too, Mr. Smaldoon," Matt said.

Smaldoon obliged him, smiling wolfishly.

Matt turned his gaze back to the two outlaws. "All right, you've got about as fair a shake as you're ever going to get. Make your move."

One of the men blurted out, his voice quivering, "I'm en- titled to a fair trial! I ain't movin' a muscle till the law gits here!"

Unfortunately, the other man decided to use his companion's panic-stricken speech as a diversion, and went for his gun.

"Aw, hell," the first man said, seeing his comrade's action, and started to draw as well.

It was too late. His friend was already dead, and it was a bare fraction of a second until he followed his erstwhile buddy.

Kincaid and Smaldoon reholstered their pistols as Weasel moved slowly across the room to where little Billy was kneeling by the body of Bull Caber. The eyes Billy turned up toward him were filled with tears.

"You kilt my pa."

"He tried to kill *you*," Weasel said softly. "And he said he warn't your pa."

"He *was* my pa!" the boy cried.

Weasel started to say something else, but then he realized that the poor kid didn't have anything left at all, and who was it going to hurt for the youngster to hang onto this one desperate belief?

Shrugging, Weasel turned and walked out of the saloon.

twenty-four ─────────

The letter from Deputy Marshal Long arrived two weeks later. He had recently arrived back in Denver, had been given the wire by his chief, and had looked into the matter. Long thought it sounded kind of personal, so he'd decided to write instead of wiring. He also figured on letting Matt take care of it; he'd met Kincaid and knew he was capable.

Matt read the letter in his office, then he came out and stuck his head into Captain Conway's office. "You got anything you want done down by Denver, sir?"

Conway stared at him from behind his desk, thought it over, and said, "Can't think of anything official, Matt. Sorry."

Ben Cohen, though, overhearing, said, "*I* can."

Matt gave him his immediate attention.

"One of that bunch we caught killin' Indians?" recalled Sgt Cohen. "Caught 'em up by Silver Fox?"

Matt nodded.

"Well, one of them's wanted down Denver way, for killin' some jasper in a saloon. We been waitin' for the law to pick 'em up, but they don't seem to be in any hurry. Like to get him off our hands. Be a good excuse, anyways."

Matt rode out with a squad and the prisoner later that day.

Early the second day following, he dropped the prisoner off in Denver. Private Malone—Matt had taken First Platoon's first squad, his usual—thought that the prisoner must have been about the most wanted man west of the Mississippi. They'd stopped a couple of times to pee, but that was about it. And by the time the prisoner got to Denver, he was looking forward to luxuriating at the end of a rope.

But still, it wasn't done with. Matt kept right on going, dragging his squad on south.

Noon found them off the main trail, up toward the mountains, pausing atop a ridge where Matt looked down on a small ranch in the narrow valley below.

"Think I found your people, Matt," the letter from Deputy Marshal Long had read, *"and if you don't mind, I think I'll let you have them. They're a mite too weird for this deputy.*

"Like you guessed, they've taken up residence on an old ranch, been abandoned for a while. Some local folk recall that it belonged to Beckwith. Apparently there were always Indians hanging around, that's how they remember.

"Couple of men there, a few women, a boy, but I could only see from a distance.

"Backtraced into Denver. I know the Beckwith story, too. Found some records of marriages real recent. But damned if I could figure out who married who. One of the ladies was named Elizabeth Ledweiler. You may recall that Jim Beckwith married a gal named Elizabeth Lettbetter, in Denver. I'll bet this Barrett fellow looked all over for a gal with the same name, but this was the closest he got. And let me tell you, he must have been determined, because this Ledweiler's an old whore and loony as hell, and hardly remembers what happened.

"Barrett, or whatever his name is, dropped her right away and moved on south. He picked up some Indian woman on the way. Don't know her name, but he probably named her Sue.

"Seems he's following the Beckwith story right on down the line. Hope he knows about Beckwith getting poisoned.

"Oh, yes, a Negro blacksmith got murdered here about that time. No one's got any idea who did it. But you will recall that Beckwith killed a colored blacksmith, too.

"Matt, my friend, you are welcome to this dude.

"Still, if you need any help, I'll be around for a while, far as I know."

Matt and his men dropped down off the ridge and slowly approached the ranch. They checked the loads in their pistols and carried their Springfields at the ready.

It looked like a garden had been planted by the side of the main house. Matt also saw some milk cows out back, and some hogs and a few head of cattle farther on down the valley. Looked like they'd settled in for a long stay.

The door of the main house opened and a tall man emerged. It wasn't Barrett.

It was Lame Dog. He regarded them steadily.

A white girl came out behind him, then a young boy and an older Indian woman. She was ugly enough to be a Crow, thought Matt.

Matt's squad spread out on either side of him, rifles leveled. Lame Dog didn't flinch.

Matt thought he'd rarely seen a taller, straighter, better-looking Indian. The man exuded pride, intelligence, and guts.

"Where is Medicine Calf?" asked Matt.

"Gone. The man you want, Barrett, follows his vision."

Damn, thought Matt, this was as far as the vision went, as far as he knew. "Who are you? What's *your* name?"

"Lame Dog, or—"

"Then I want you too. Sorry."

"—or Leonard Dugan," completed Lame Dog.

The white girl giggled.

Matt frowned.

"My wife," said Lame Dog, or Leonard Dugan. "Alicia. And her brother . . . and a Sparrowhawk woman"—he seemed to become a trifle embarrassed—"named Sue."

"Holy moley, sir," exclaimed Malone, his rifle drooping.

No wonder Deputy Marshal Long didn't want to have anything to do with this, thought Matt—and he probably didn't know the half of it.

"Leonard Dugan, huh?" he muttered. "Where's the other girl?"

"Barrett let her go," said Lame Dog.

"She rode off in a wagon with some people going north," said Alicia. "She wanted to go . . . home."

"And you?" asked Matt. "You want to stay here?"

"Yes. Me and my brother, we want to stay with Leonard."

Matt didn't understand it. "They killed your folks," he said. "*He* didn't."

Matt realized he was dealing with a simple girl, goodhearted and forgiving, who knew she had nothing to go back to except some distant relatives and the wickedly cold Montana winters. And he could understand the appeal of the handsome, noble Lame Dog—or Leonard Dugan or whoever.

"And I got a baby comin', too."

"Oh, *shit*!" exploded Matt, and he turned his horse and rode off, the squad following.

They spent a couple of days in Denver. Dobbs, Malone, and Rottweiler got incredibly drunk. Holzer and Miller made sure

169

Dobbs, Malone, and Rottweiler didn't get into any trouble, or at least no more trouble than they could handle. Parker, Medwick, Weatherby, and Carter spent part of the time fighting and the rest of the time licking their wounds.

Two and a half days later, along about midnight, Matt Kincaid and the squad rode back into Outpost Number Nine.

Matt had barely dismounted when Windy approached him, which was surprising since Windy usually spent his nights comforting maidens over at the friendlies' village. "There's a feller waitin' for you in town, Matt."

"Barrett?"

" 'Bout at the end of his rope, Matt."

Matt stood by his horse, thinking. He said, almost to himself, "These men are too tired." Then, raising his voice, he told Windy, "Roust out Sergeant Chubb for me, and Enright. Tell them to pack for a little trip, maybe."

He then walked off to find and talk to Captain Conway.

Several men leaned against the bar in the Drovers Rest. Riffraff, mostly, a couple of mean-faced hardcases and the clerk from the general store, whose night it was to drink late.

"Ain't I seen that dude sittin' back there?" said one of the town riffraff, eyeing a man sitting deep in the shadows to the rear of the saloon.

"Looks like the dude what had the fight with Harvey an' them."

"It is," said the clerk, seizing his moment in the spotlight, even though he wasn't comfortable with his companions and preferred some quiet drinking.

" 'Cept *that* dude was a sojer" one of the townies said.

"No, that's him," declared the clerk. "I was there."

"Well, shit!" exclaimed another in a hoarse whisper. "Then that's the dude what's a nigger that thinks he's Injun an' led them Crow jumpers, which was *after* he killed an' scalped pore ol' Harvey an' them."

The hardcases suddenly took an interest in the conversation.

But it was one of the last speaker's buddies who sneered, "Aw, shit, Willy, where'd you hear *that*?"

"Out t' the sutler's, on the post. *Ever'body* out there knows it."

"You mean," said one of the hardcases, "that dude back there's a nigger and a Injun and a killer?"

170

"Yep," cried Willy, "all three of them, he sure is."

"An' he's jes' sittin' aroun' free as a bird?"

"Don't seem right, does it?"

Matt Kincaid told Chubb and Enright to wait for him outside. Then he walked into the Drovers Rest.

It was dimly lit, late, and there weren't many men around. There was a group at the bar, but so few others that the saloon girls had already called it a night. Whitey stood behind the bar, listlessly wiping glasses.

Matt peered into the gloom at the rear of the saloon. A man was seated back there.

Matt walked toward the rear, past the bar against which the group of men sagged. Whitey looked up, saw him, and tried to catch his eye, but failed.

Barrett stood up as Matt approached. "Hello, Matt," he said, adding with a smile, "sir."

"Private Barrett."

Barrett shook his head. "Medicine Calf."

"As you wish."

"There's yet a chapter."

Matt didn't know about any other chapter. He hadn't read that far. But he couldn't have read what hadn't been written. "Don't," he said. "Don't do anything more. Just let me take you back."

Barrett shook his head again. "You never give up, do you?"

"Nope. Too many people have died on account of you and your damned visions."

"Have you read the Bible? The white man's Bible?"

"Naturally."

"Yes . . . naturally." Barrett smiled. "You may recall that when Jesus was on the cross and saying things, the wise men were amazed because he was intent on fulfilling the prophecies."

"I do seem to recall something like that."

"Well, the prophecy shall be fulfilled. . . ."

"Barrett," groaned Matt, "for Christ's sake, why don't you just pack it in, let me take you back—"

"You're going to have to kill me, Matt."

"The hell I am. Look, I can take you back, then send you off to—I don't know, some hospital, or someplace like that."

"No. You're wrong. I'd just be hanged, and that's not the way I want it to end." He stared at Matt. "But if you won't fight me, won't kill me, then I guess you're just going to have to catch me."

He stood up suddenly and turned toward the back door.

"Bar—" Matt began, but his voice was drowned out by the thunder of sixguns from somewhere behind him.

Barrett spun in a full circle, then fell.

Matt lifted himself slowly out of his chair and turned around.

"Is he dead?" cried one of the gents at the bar. "That was that bastard Injun what killed my buddies. Didn't you know that? He was gittin' away."

"No, he wasn't," said Matt, his voice hollow. He fought to comprehend what had just happened. Rage began to build in him.

Wisps of smoke curled from the barrel of the man's Colt. The two hardcases flanked him, their lips drawn back in cruel, hard smiles, their hands hanging by their holstered Colts. One of them sneered, "Whyn't you jes' take a walk, sojer boy, go shine up yer leather real good."

Whitey the barkeep, hearing that, began slowly to duck down behind the bar.

"He's still movin'!" cried the man who had nailed Barrett. "I'm gonna finish that son of a bitch off." He started toward the rear of the saloon.

Matt stepped in his way. "Put that gun away," he said softly, so softly that one might have thought he didn't want the man to obey.

"The hell I will," the gent snorted. "Git outta my way or I'll do you the same's I done him. Now *git*!"

The hardcases had edged closer.

The pistol held by Barrett's would-be killer was pointed at Matt's belly, and his face was a mask of hatred. Maybe he deserved to die, maybe he didn't, but Matt couldn't stop the rage.

It takes a good part of a second for a man to see something—in this case, Matt's lightning cross-draw—have it register in his brain, and then send the message down to his own hand, the message being, *"Pull the goddamn trigger."*

It takes longer still if a man's had a couple of drinks. And the message was still just streaking down his arm when Matt's exploding Scoff started blowing him away.

Three slugs Matt put in him—the man never did get to pull the trigger. Two more slugs nailed one of the hardcases in mid-draw. The other one did get his gun out, but only shot a couple of holes in the floor as he was going down.

His twitching body hadn't even come to rest before Matt was turning away to bend over Barrett. He saw blood coming from the corner of the man's mouth.

"Gut," whispered Barrett. "Lung."

Matt bent close. And Barrett whispered a request. It was what Matt thought it might be.

Yet he sat back on his haunches and stared straight ahead for a long while before he finally looked down and nodded.

Kincaid and Chubb and Enright loaded the still-living Barrett onto a horse, tying him into the saddle.

"How bad is he, sir?" asked Enright.

Matt took him and Chubb aside. "Not all that bad," he said. "Might recover with a lot of nursing. But he'd just get hanged."

They mounted up and rode northwest.

By some act of will, Barrett was still living when they stopped by the Wind River to pick some tobacco plants; they were not nearly grown, but close enough.

But he became delirious as they climbed up into Yellowstone Park and followed the Yellowstone River down into Montana. By then Chubb and Enright were nearly delirious, too. What had *they* done to deserve this?

Barrett died before they reached the Crow reservation, but still they rode.

White Moccasin met them, and together they built a platform by the Big Boulder River, where, according to White Moccasin, Medicine Calf had received his decisive vision, his marching orders, and they placed Barrett/Bloody Arm/Medicine Calf atop the platform along with his rifle, his guns, a war hatchet, and whatever robes they could find.

"Hell," swore Sergeant Chubb, "with all these damn 'skeeters, no wonder he had a vision." He was slapping at them like a madman. "Drive *anyone* nuts."

They smoked the tobacco at the base of the platform.

White Moccasin said Barrett's horse should be slain, to accompany him.

Matt rebelled. He wasn't about to slaughter a horse. There'd been enough slaughtering. He suspected, though, that as soon as he and his men were gone, a pony would be killed. And there wasn't much he could do to stop that.

* * *

Back at Outpost Number Nine, Matt sent a message to Lame Dog, telling of the events that had transpired. It was right that he should know.

Then Matt had to explain to Captain Conway why he'd had to kill all those men in town.

Conway made him tell it twice, just to get the facts straight. And besides, he enjoyed hearing it. "Told you to go shine up your leather, did he?"

Weasel Gillies sat across the parade, in front of the barracks, whittling.

He stared across at the orderly room. Enright had told everyone the story. Weasel sure wished he'd been there alongside Lieutenant Kincaid.

Matt came out of the orderly room and stood looking over the parade, hooking his thumbs in his belt and breathing deep. Weasel had to squint, watching him; the sun was bright.

"Sure musta been some shootout," said a voice at his shoulder.

He looked around.

Billy Caber looked at him, his eyes steady and serious. Weasel hadn't seen him since the day he'd killed Bull Caber.

"Billy," said Weasel. Then, "Goddammit, Billy, I do believe you've grown some."

Billy grinned.

The following spring, Matt Kincaid visited the Crow reservation. The platform remained, but the bones were gone and White Moccasin would not say where they'd been placed. But the old Indian did show him a space where tobacco had been planted and would surely grow. Which meant the Absaroka, as a people, would survive, would not pass from the face of the earth.

Matt Kincaid hoped that he was right. But it wasn't something he'd care to bet on.

Sure, they'd kept the bones and spirit of Jim Beckwith, and now they had the bones and spirit of the madman, Barrett. But it might be that they were going to need more than the spirit and strength of both men, no matter how powerful their medicine might have been, to see them safely along the white man's path.

SPECIAL PREVIEW

Here are the opening scenes
from

EASY COMPANY AND THE LONGHORNS

the next novel in Jove's exciting
new High Plains adventure series

EASY COMPANY

coming in June!

one _____

There was a certain ungainliness about them, those almost pathetic creatures with the pointed beards, hairy forebodies, and bare rumps, whose rounded, short horns curled ineffectually from the sides of their heads and to a point before their eyes. Long, stringy, matted hair hung from their chests behind stubby front legs, and it nearly touched the tall grass as they grazed warily across the prairies in the semiprotected swale provided by two rolling ridges joined at an oblique angle. The buffalo, their yellow eyes constantly searching above the feast as tufts of grass were munched in powerful jaws, moved unsuspectingly forward with the wind to their backs. The field of green shifted before them like undulating waves on an endless sea. Calves frolicked at their mother's sides, oblivious to time and danger, while the bulls raised their heads with every mouthful and searched the wind for some alien sight or scent that might indicate danger and send them scampering away with speed apparently uncharacteristic of their misshapen torsos.

But the sun, angling toward the horizon on those northern plains, revealed a signal of which the buffalo were unaware. Five blued rifle barrels glinted dully as they were aimed downward, motionless now and waiting silently for the herd of seventy-five animals to graze within range.

Lying flat on his stomach, with a chew of tobacco working noiselessly beneath his unshaven, bristly cheek, Samuel "Hoss" Boggs squinted down his rifle barrel while traces of brown saliva glistened at the corners of his mouth. His wide-brimmed

177

hat, pulled low to his eyes and soiled with sweat stains, covered a wild shock of red hair that bulged out beneath the black leather hat and covered his ears in an unruly tangle. To his left were two of his sons, leering-eyed men who also squinted along warm steel, their fingers fairly itching for the pull of the trigger and the slamming jolt of a bullet being sent with a thudding smack into the bodies of the animals below. Daniel and Martin Boggs, twenty-three and twenty-four respectively, thought much like their father in that they believed the buffalo were nothing more than vermin to be exterminated from valuable rangeland better used to sustain the Double G cattle herds:

But off to his left, sweat trickling down his forehead, lay Timothy Boggs, eighteen and uncomfortable in the thought of the carnage that awaited. Clean-shaven and lacking the thick, massive body of his father and brothers, Timmy was tall and lean, with blond hair, and his upper lip was graced by the faintest wisp of a mustache. His eyes drifted to the rock-still figure of his father, who continued to stare downward and silently work the bulge in his cheek. There was an uncomfortableness in Timmy's eyes as they went back to the sights again, and he sighed as he shifted the rifle to a more comfortable position.

"Whatsamatter, boy?" Jake Barnes whispered thickly. "Got no stomach for this kind of work?"

Timmy's hat tilted with the slight shake of his head as he glanced over at the ranch foreman. Barnes was a man of medium height, barrel-chested, with thick, sloping shoulders supporting a bull-like neck and an ugly head. He had a wide gap between his front teeth. His beady, darting eyes matched the twisted sneer of his mouth. Barnes had a well-earned reputation for being one of the meanest, cruelest, and most unforgiving of all the barroom brawlers and gutter fighters ever produced in West Texas. And, as Timmy watched him, he again noticed the ragged scar where the lower portion of Barnes' left ear had been bitten off in one such fight. And he remembered the story of the conclusion of that brawl, in which Barnes had killed his opponent with a knife slash across the throat and then severed the dead man's ear and stuffed it into his mouth. "If you've got such a hunger for ears," Barnes had been reported as saying, "then here's a little somethin' for ya to nibble on in hell, ya miserable son of a bitch!"

Timmy felt a cold chill tickle up his spine, despite the heat. "No, Jake," he replied, "I'm not much for—"

An angry "Ssshhhh!"—coming from the elder Boggs—silenced the two men. "I'll drop that lead bull," Boggs said in a coarse whisper, without taking his eyes from the sights, "and the rest of you pick off the other bulls, especially the ones that look to run. Then we'll shoot the calves and cows. Should be able to get the whole damned bunch. Easy now, about ten more steps and we've got 'em."

There was silence on the plains, save for the whisper of shifting grass in the increasing wind and the occasional bleat of a calf that had strayed too far from its mother's side. Then a booming shot split the calm, and the lead bull went to its knees and flopped over on one side as though suddenly desirous of sleep induced by a .44-caliber bullet smacking into its head just behind the right ear.

Instantly, three other rifles spat their deadly poison and three more bulls crumpled in silent, almost obedient death. The remaining buffalo raised their heads with grass yet munching in their jaws, and watched their leaders with more curiosity than concern. Again, four rifles fired from above, and other animals on the periphery of the herd went down, the victims of well-aimed shots intended to kill instantly. Strangely, it was only the calves who showed alarm in their tail-high scampering to seek out their mother's protection. The slain animals had crumpled in the grass with nothing more than the occasional twitch of a stiffening leg, and since mature buffalo reacted only to alarm demonstrated by their leaders, which was not forthcoming in this case, they lowered their heads and again began to graze.

The shots from the high ground were well spaced now, and as quickly as one animal went down, another from the opposite side of the herd followed suit, until all the bulls were dead and the weapons were turned on cows and calves with less concern for deadly accuracy. But still, one rifle had not fired.

Hoss Boggs rolled onto one side to jam fresh cartridges into his Henry, and his hands worked with mechanical precision while his grayish-blue eyes glared at his youngest son. "Damn you, Timothy," he said with a menacing growl, "let's put some heat down that barrel!"

Timmy continued to stare down his sights, but his trigger finger was motionless and his only movement was another

179

slight shake of his head. "Don't cotton to killing healthy animals for nothing, Pa," he said cautiously, knowing the outburst that would follow.

"I don't give a goddamn what you cotton to, boy!" Boggs snapped in an enraged whisper. "And don't you never talk back to me, hear? Now I'm gonna watch you from right here, and the next buff that goes down is gonna fall to your gun." Boggs' eyes snapped to what was left of the herd, then back to Timmy. "Take that little feller there, the one trying to snatch a pull from his momma's tit."

Timmy looked toward the calf, but did not aim his rifle in that direction.

"I said take him, boy," Boggs warned, his voice ominous and threatening.

Slowly, Tommy's rifle barrel swung toward the calf while spaced shots continued on either side of him, and he saw more buffalo falling from the corners of his eyes. His sights lined up on the little animal, whose neck was arched beneath his mother's flank. His finger tightened on the trigger, but he hesitated.

"I said take him, Timothy. And don't miss. I know what kind of shot you are when you want to be. Take him, boy, and take him now!"

Timmy hesitated a moment longer, then the rifle belched flame and the tiny calf slammed into its mother's hind legs as the slug smashed through its heart. Boggs twisted, raised his rifle, and instantly the mother was dead as well.

"Nice shot," Boggs grunted, his eyes searching the herd for another target. "Had to get her quick, she mighta spooked the rest of the herd. Now keep shootin', boy. I didn't buy that rifle for you to use as a crutch."

In a space of ten minutes the entire herd lay strewn across the prairie floor in motionless lumps, with the sighing wind twisting the hair across their backs in restless surges. The ridge was silent and the men lay their hot rifles in the grass to cool while they collected the brass cartridges scattered about them. Timmy could feel his father's searing eyes on his face as he picked up a mere four spent rounds, which he stuffed quietly into his vest pocket.

"Four shots, boy? Is that all you fired? Four lousy, chicken-shit shots?"

Timmy nodded without looking at his father. "Guess so, Pa."

"Guess so? You damned well *know* so! Why?"

Barnes grinned as he massaged the gap between his teeth with a blade of grass. "Looks like the young feller ain't got much of a stomach for killin', Hoss."

Timmy glanced once at Barnes, then across at his father. "Jake's right, Pa. I ain't got much stomach for killin'. Especially when it's senseless, like that was."

The men were standing now, and Boggs' massive chest bulged beneath his cotton shirt and strained against the two buttons holding it close over his distended but rock-hard stomach. "Senseless?" He spat viciously and took a menacing step toward his son. "You callin' what I order to be done senseless?"

Timmy watched his father's clublike hands forming into fists by his sides. His eyes went to the elder man's face, and the muscles worked along his jaw as he clenched his teeth. "Yeah, Pa, I am," he said softly. "Those buffalo weren't hurtin'—"

With flashing speed beyond what one would expect of a man so huge, Samuel Boggs' fist cracked across his son's chin in a glancing blow, and Timmy staggered backward but did not go down. Hurt filled his eyes and a tiny trickle of blood dripped from the corner of his mouth, but he seemed not to notice as he continued to stare at his father, whose rage had now grown to nearly uncontrollable fury.

"Those buffalo was eatin' Double G grass, that's what they was doin' wrong! They're nothin' but vermin and deserve to be shot like a damned coyote or prairie dog. We've got to protect our rangeland for our cattle, and 'sides that, a buff will mount a cow in heat quicker'n a fly'll come to shit. Don't want no buff blood in my herd, just like I don't want no backtalk from my sons!"

Off to one side, Daniel and Martin Boggs had been watching their father in apprehensive silence, and now their eyes drifted down to stare at the grass between their boots. But Timmy did not look away.

"This is our land, is it, Pa?" he asked softly. "Seems to me like the Arapaho were here first."

"Arapaho? Buffalo? Who gives a shit? One ain't no better'n the other."

Boggs' eyes closed to narrow, squinting slits. "This is government land, boy, and that makes it our land, what we can take of it, that is. When the buffalo are gone, the Indians will be, as well, and the government's given us permission to do that little trick. Even asked us to. What we're doin' is patriotic, somethin' for our country." His lips curled into a sudden, yellow-toothed smile, and he spoke to Barnes while continuing to stare at his son. "Ain't that right, Jake?"

"Right as rain, Hoss. When it came time to wave the flag, ain't neither of us had a slow hand."

Boggs' guffaw rolled across the silent land. "True for a fact." Then his lips went straight and his voice lowered to a sad tone. "You're different from the rest of us, Timothy. Yer ma done that by sendin' ya off to school, God rest her ignorant soul. Yer brothers is like me, but yer like yer ma. Too soft, too kind for Plains life. But I'll whip some toughness into ya, mind me I will."

"Maybe you will, Pa, but you'll be the loser if you do."

"You talkin' back to me again, boy?"

"No, Pa. Just telling you the truth."

"Truth, huh? Only truth is you got blood running out of yer mouth fer sass and you let me down today more'n any man could. Now wipe yer face clean and go get the horses. We got work to do back at the ranch."

Timmy continued to stare at his father for several seconds before stooping, snatching his hat from the ground, and moving toward the distant grove with long, proud strides.

Boggs watched him go and shook his head sadly. "Damn her fool hide," he muttered through gritted teeth. "I ain't got no time nor need for weaklings. She done that to him."

Barnes had begun slowly to jam fresh shells into his rifle, and he looked up from his work. "Maybe she did, Hoss. Maybe she did. Then again, maybe he's just made that way."

"Made that way my ass, Jake. He's my blood. His sister's got more spunk than he has."

Jake Barnes continued to watch Boggs' face, and there was no fear in his eyes. "You're wrong, Hoss. He's got half his ma's blood too. And as for Jennie, she's got more spunk than she's a right to, to my way a' thinkin'."

A glower came over Boggs' face again. "You talkin' down about my daughter, Jake?"

Again, Barnes' face was an expressionless mask of uncon-cern as he stared at the larger man. "No, Samuel, I'm not. Facts is facts. If they weren't, she wouldn't be bedded down with a gambler in Texas right now."

"You ain't nobody to be short-shootin' gamblers, Jake,"

Boggs said. "You've lost more money at poker than any man I know."

"That I have. And I've bedded a lot of women just like Jennie."

They stared at each other for nearly a minute before Boggs spun on his heel, turning toward his other sons. "You two go down there and cut the backstrap out of one of them cows. Might as well have a dinner off of 'em if nothin' else."

Daniel and Martin moved away in obedient silence, and Boggs watched them pull knives from their belts as they walked down the hill. "Now them's the kinda boys a man needs, Jake," he said pridefully. "Never say nothin', do what they're told, and don't ask no questions."

Barnes watched them as well, and nodded his agreement. "You're right and you're wrong, Hoss. Timmy's got more man in him than either of them, but the part about askin' questions is true for a fact. Seems like there ain't always time for answers."

Unseen by the two stockmen, lying flat on the adjoining prairie rise, a man moved backward in the grass and the single feather in his hair rustled with the breeze. A magnificent spotted pony stood patiently at the bottom of the hill on the far side of the rise, and when he knew he could not be seen, Black Wing stood and moved toward his mount in a hunched-over trot. When he swung onto the horse's back, he glanced once more toward the crest. There was hatred in his eyes combined with the defiant look of a warrior, angry and prepared for battle. There was a wild handsomeness about him, mixed with the deadly countenance of a rattlesnake coiled and ready to strike. Finally, Black Wing touched a moccasined heel to his pony's flank and raced across the plains toward the distant hills.